*The Walter Integral* is Walter Smith's first novel. He and his wife, Fran, live in Wellington, Florida, and New Canaan CT. Walter received his BS and Ph.D. from Rensselaer Polytechnic Institute and has spent more than forty years as an entrepreneur, consultant, inventor, and owner of several science-related businesses.

To past, present, and future members of the Smith family.

# Walter Smith

# THE WALTER INTEGRAL

## Year of the Not Quite Depend™ Adult Undergarment

AUSTIN MACAULEY PUBLISHERS™

LONDON • CAMBRIDGE • NEW YORK • SHARJAH

**Ordering Information:**
Quantity sales: special discounts are available on quantity purchases by corporations, associations, and others. For details, contact the publisher at the address below.

**Publisher's Cataloging-in-Publication data**
Smith, Walter
The Walter Integral

ISBN 9781645750574 (Paperback)
ISBN 9781645750567 (Hardback)
ISBN 9781645750598 (ePub e-book)

Library of Congress Control Number: 2020912386

www.austinmacauley.com/us

First Published (2020)
Austin Macauley Publishers LLC
40 Wall Street, 28th Floor
New York, NY 10005
USA

mail-usa@austinmacauley.com
+1 (646) 5125767

Thanks to Jarrod and Chelsea for providing the impetus to read *real* literature most notably *Infinite Jest*. Thanks to my wife Fran and daughter Jesse, for more than they can possibly imagine. A special thanks to both Jon P and Jeff G, each providing critical commentary and encouragement throughout the writing process.

# Table of Contents

# The Integral

The Integral of *The Walter Integral* doesn't refer to the common definition, that as defined by Merriam-Webster as being 'an essential part thereof', but rather the Riemann Integral or the anti-derivative, this being a mathematical term essential to the development of both advanced mathematics and calculus. For those with a mathematical bent, an integral, in this case a definite integral, can be simply and precisely defined as 'the area under a curve defined by a function, $f(x)$, and the curve being bounded by a minimal value of $x$ and a maximal value as well.'

However for the most, simply spoke, an integral or integration actually, the verb form, is a way of calculating a total by adding together tiny slices of a bigger picture. In this case, each slice is a moment in time, a tableau, and their integration results in a bio, a portrait, or a not quite complete picture of our main character.

# Part 0

## Author's Notes and Homage to David Foster Wallace

As a reader and I'm definitely more of a reader than a writer, prologues, in fact, pretty much anything, pre-story longer than a paragraph is something I generally skip, my thinking, let's get on to the tale, if I've missed something important, I can always backtrack. However, this short introduction is quite important, as how often is a somewhat lengthy clarification needed to help understand a title, a subtitle, and the subtitle leading into an homage? Are you ready for a somewhat tortuous journey involving the elaboration of abstract concepts, seldom discussed mathematical, biological, and otherworldly scientific topics, jumps back and forth through time and copious footnotes leading into other dimensions and origami folds of the lead character of this narrative? Let's hope so!

While direct, simple, and straightforward, might get one to their desired destination, the final stop, or ultimate resting place, perhaps, in doing so, in taking this most direct passage, unlimited possibilities, alternative realities and existences, perhaps, far more exciting ones, are missed, a whole 'nother' world in fact, lost forever. Taking such a detour and not following the norm, or the acceptable path, and being forced to deal with the consequences of such choices is a reoccurring theme we will see throughout this journey.

*The Walter Integral* is about baseball, it is about childhood, it is about adolescent obesity, and it is about random and unexpected events forever affecting personal growth and development. It is about wild accusations doing the same and perhaps, more significantly so. It is about recreational drug usage, it is about sex, and it is about family and the securities, often completely unrealistic, and the insecurities that familial interactions have to beget! It is about that enriching, perhaps troublesome, confusing for sure, time of life we call college; it is about youth sports, baseball, bowling, and golf, and it ponders and examines free will or the lack of, and in coming to a conclusion it is about playing the hand you have been dealt, doing so optimistically, delusional, as well, may work, making the most you can with those cards, and moving on and just being. Being better, being stronger, being surer. Yes, it is a coming of age narrative, but more than that; perhaps, it might be a real bildungsroman or as you get to know Walter, you might even consider this to be a picaresque novel. This saga, this creation is simply a story, one viewed from several slices or integrals, not being the complete picture!

This narrative is, also, an homage and if not for the posthumous influence of David Foster Wallace, *The Walter Integral* would not exist. DFW's influence will become all more apparent as you continue this journey, especially for those readers of his regrettably far too abbreviated body of work. The role of Depends™ is the heart and lungs of this narrative, a word overused by DFW, narrative is the overused word, neither heart nor lungs were overused by DFW, hideous, perhaps also, and this author as well.

In his masterpiece, '*Infinite Jest*', Wallace takes today's real and obscene commercialism and corporate sponsorship to an unpredictable absurdity. In our real world of today, we are all far too familiar with this corporate insanity, especially, the renaming of events and sporting arenas after corporate 'partners.' Baseball parks are being renamed and it now seems on an ever-accelerating pace, in fact almost daily. Because of this sponsorship, almost all of us, including those who are not fans of the game, must know that Shea Stadium is now Citi Field, and Tigers Stadium is Comerica Park. In Chicago, Comiskey Park has been arguably adorned with the worse name ever, 'Guaranteed Rate Field', really, and in San Francisco the former Candlestick Park has been serially renamed, Bell Park, SBC Park, and currently, bears the moniker AT & T Park; at least, for now, Fenway Park and Yankee Stadium remain true to their heritage, although the Boston Garden, well let's just skip that.

In '*Infinite Jest*' the rampant promulgation of commercialism is such that years are no longer numbered but named (subsidized time), the year being named after a commercial product that was designated by the corporate entity making the highest bid for the veneration of naming the year. Wallace describes in his story a very provocative yet captivating year, in which the narrative switches between, intersecting, expertly crafted drug related stories, concerning a rehab house in suburban Boston and events at a fictitious Boston private school, devoted to the development of tennis prodigies, of which DFW and the fictional lead character of his narrative, undoubtedly based upon himself, was one or, perhaps, two; in his tale, the year (Wallace scholars believe it is actually 2009) is not numerical but is dubbed The Year of the Depend™ Adult Undergarment; clearly Kimberly-Clark made the best offer for sponsorship in that fictional year.

DFW was also known for the immeasurable and sometimes, distracting or just plain annoying use of footnotes; therefore, in laudation, and not only as a triviality or as a panegyric to DFW, this narrative will also rely on the use of footnotes, to open hidden chapters and explore other dimensions and memories of the lead character, Walter the Younger. And readers, although they, the footnotes, are distracting and cumbersome, please read them as they are integral to *The Walter Integral* and *yes*, pun intended.

But why choose the year named Depend™ the Adult Undergarment? As you press-on in this journey that connection will become blindingly clear, if, in fact, it hasn't already and has nothing to do with tennis, Boston, nor a drug rehab clinic.

# Part 1

## Little League, Uncle Al,
## and other adventures

There were no Depend™ Adult Undergarments or any other similar products designed for use by anyone older than the age of three or four, size-dependent of course, when Walter played Little League baseball from 1960 to 1963.[1] It was

---

[1] Throughout this narrative, the trademark designation for any and all references to Little League Baseball will not be used. The term 'Little League' and the league itself was created in 1939 in Williamsport PA, as we all now know, thanks to ESPN, ESPN 2, ESPN News, ESPN streaming etc., etc., by Carl Stolz and his wife; this fact you probably did not know. Although having no children of their own, Carl and his wife were obviously excited about, perhaps obsessed with youth baseball, community spirit, and such very good, goody stuff, as sportsmanship, giving your best etc., and please don't read in sarcasm here as there is none and along with the help of friends and family started the first Little League league, the first game in this league being played in Williamsport, PA, of course, with Lundy Lumber defeating Lycoming Dairy 23-8, clearly a no ten-run rule back in the day. Today, there are an estimated three million boys and now, girls, aged nine to twelve, and in some cases, thirteen and even sixteen-

unlikely large personal care companies were even looking into such a crazy idea at that time. Depend™ Adult Undergarments were introduced to the US market in 1984, a Brainiac idea, demographics driven, from the Kimberly-Clark Corporation. Depends™ now have more than a thirty-year history of successful marketing and worldwide sales, a very visible public image and mainline media exposure. TV, Facebook, social media, and print ads abound. In fact, today, former NFL super-stars and Super Bowl Champions, with thinning pates, thickening waistlines, and very likely undiagnosed CTE, these traits seemingly not fitting the images we, so dearly, hold onto of these heroes, those images enshrined in our memory, frozen in the permafrost of time, fossilized, they, as exemplars of triumph, nevertheless, these now less than super humans they are now us, everyman, un-superstars, are unabashedly hawking this product and countless others, for who knows how much money. Clearly, in the now, there is no shame in being a little bit leaky.

---

year old's playing Little League ball, the older and ineligible players participating simply because winning local, regional, state, national, and world titles has become such an important business, and well, it is just worth the risk to cheat. Little League is capitalized and not a generic term, since on July 17, 1964 President Lyndon Johnson, granted Little League baseball a Federal Charter, far better than a trademark and much harder to get. Of those granted charters the list includes, the Boy and Girl Scouts of America and the American Red Cross. Protected, yes, these organizations are and far more protected and special than simply being awarded a trade mark designation!

As long as the money is good! [2]

Depend™ Adult Undergarments, during their early years of existence and commercialization, and long after when Walter desperately needed them during his Little League adventures, were likely hidden away on the back shelves of your local pharmacy, and if you just happened to search for such products in that aforementioned pharmacy, unquestionably, they would have been difficult to find, inconveniently located next to the wart removal products as well as other 'unmentionables.' Perhaps, near the fire exits and also in close proximity to the employee's lounge; they might have also been neighboring the customer restrooms, but these were not so common nor legislated by local laws or zoning regulations in the mid-1980s. Come to think of it, positioning near the restrooms would make sense. There were no Walmart's™ or any superstores in this past time we are speaking of. Local, independent pharmacies, likely owned by a prominent member of your small town and likely known to all, was the norm. But today, most of these small, independents have vanished, replaced by the massive omnipresent, omni-purveyors used by all, each and every one of us to binge shop and why not, since with just a push of your cart, toiletries are available aisle six, wine aisle ten, gourmet food aisle twelve, infant-wear aisle thirteen, adult diapers, also, aisle thirteen, bedding and bath, electronics, shoes, auto supplies, computer and office supplies, Harry and David's™ tasty treats, lawnmowers, golf equipment, even golf carts, guns, ammo, fishing equipment, fish, pets,

---

[2] The adult undergarment market is projected to reach $20 billion in worldwide sales in 2020.

furniture, flowers, cut and living, shrubs, trees, and more. You can redecorate your kitchen, cabinets, counter tops, natural and synthetic, flooring, hardware, appliances, sinks, and faucets. You can buy garage doors, install new hurricane proof windows, upgrade your washer and dryer; you can get pretty much anything you want for the home and garden; and why go to the doctor, you can take your blood pressure, buy your corrective lenses, get a flu shot or other vaccination; shingles, herpes zoster, the vaccination *du jour*, the human papilloma virus vaccine and the pneumococcal vaccine, pretty much universally recommended today; create a vaccine and then convince the public this is what they have been missing for all those years when such ailments were largely ignored, all while your spouse can enjoy a hot dog, pretzel, or pizza slice for less than two dollars. *No*, these stores did not exist in this past time.

*Yes*, in the early years of Depend™ Adult Undergarments promotion they would have been difficult to find. A pressing need to acquire such a product, until recently, where one can buy almost anything with anonymity and may I add blessed anonymity and isolation, no human contact required, would likely have resulted in an extremely embarrassing encounter, perhaps, the following scenario playing out.

"Excuse me, youngster, where are the Depend™ Adult Undergarments, of course, I'm buying them for my octogenarian dad, who just recently it seems to have developed a problem and is soiling his damn khaki's?"

The pimply eighteen-year-old clerk, perhaps, a future Walter, let's forget the time disparity, would seize upon this unlikely event, wherein, he or she, more likely a he, could take the superior position and inflict whatever embarrassment he/she, 83% chance of being a he, just a guess, could upon the somewhat hesitant potential customer, a rare opportunity indeed, for such a nerd-ish youngster, as it was quite likely only a somewhat geek-ish and nerdy teen would be working the night shift at that local pharmacy, trying to earn some bucks and stow it away for an anticipated four year stint at some local and not very good state sponsored college.

"Oh, your dad, you say," eyebrows raised, a half-smile, condescension abounds, or is it condensation I'm striving for. It is quite likely this nerd-ish teen was still not completely comfortable with this encounter and in fact, some moist droplets had settled upon his forehead and upper lip, a poker player was not in the future for this young pharmacy clerk, "Please, follow me they are quite hard to find."

However, the Younger would soon need those unavailable Depends™, since his father, the elder Walter, arriving home quite late, a little unsteady, he was using pretty much any vertical surface he bumped into for support, he obviously had a few drinks, a few drinks too many, it was after nine, only a few minutes after, and on a Tuesday, typically, at least Monday through Friday, he did follow a pretty regular schedule, leave work at 5:20 p.m., avoid the downtown traffic, not really traffic at all in today's sense of the word, arrive home 5:32 p.m., down his first gin, Gordon's gin, and tonic, ice and lime, or lemon, whatever was convenient, a few cubes of slightly frosty and tasting of garlic ice[3] at 5:33 p.m. had important news to tell the family. He staggered somewhat through the front and only house entrance, leading directly into the kitchen, and after stabilizing his five-foot eight-inch frame against the entry wall, left side, he informed the entire immediate family, including mom, younger Walter, and his older sister, that after work, he, along with a number of locals, community pillars, no doubt, had attended the organizational meeting for the 1960 New Apley Little League and had laid out plans for the coming season. The meeting was held at one of the umpteen named 'clubs', another word for private bars that were in existence, for many years in fact, but since the end of WWII, these venues had become far more popular and had established themselves as important social, political-cum-watering-holes. Many meaningful and consequential small-town decisions were made in these smoke-filled and gin and beer infused meetings, typically, taking place in a large, unadorned one room building, with a long bar set in the back, perhaps, a pool table or two, an assortment of small tables and chairs, none matching and often providing illumination were brightly lit signs in neon and even more exotic colors advertising the benefits of, perhaps a Genny Cream Ale over a cool Narragansett lager. No women were invited or attended of course, even the bartender and servers were all male, it would be absurd even to consider what role the wives or girlfriends, as such domestic slaves, could or would play in 1960s rural, lower-socioeconomic class

---

[3] Does anybody know why old slightly dehydrated ice cubes have a garlic-like taste. Am I the only one who has noticed this? Is it my Italian heritage?

*Americana.* These were places where the returned soldiers, granted this was fifteen years after the end of the war, WWII, but things change slowly in small town *America*, were now experiencing a new life, a life with new responsibilities, roles had changed, decisions had to be made. The simple life of following orders was gone, these ex-soldiers were now experiencing a very different stress and battle fatigue, that being the drudgery and encumbrance of everyday life. Here, at these private clubs, these vertebrae of their families and community could gather together, relive their glory days; this reenactment consisted mostly of the telling of unquestionably aggrandized stories of these former soldiers drinking or screwing or fucking with their bosses and staying alive stories, and celebrate the fact they had indeed survived, the prodigal sons had returned and as asserted and advanced in the Bible, "They went forth and propagated." The actual Biblical reference being, "Be fruitful and multiply, increase greatly on the earth and multiply in it," since if you were at the Little League organizational meeting, there was no doubt you had a son aged 9-12.[4]

Younger Walter, then, nine, hastened to the kitchen area to join the family, as he was likely reading, escaping into one of his many different worlds of fiction, basking in what he, then and even, now, often calls 'the sunshine of isolation', in his private, but not quite so, lair, that lair being what the entire Stafford family called the 'bird's room'

---

[4] Discussion for later, now, in 2019, with more than seven and a half billion earthly human inhabitants; perhaps, we should reconsider this age-old missive!

when his dad finally rolled in. The entire family, *sans* the younger Walter, had been gathered together for quite a while in the kitchen area and was somewhat anxiously awaiting the Elder's arrival, since Dad had not informed any family member as to his possible diversion from the typical 5:33 p.m. gin schedule.

It, the 'bird's room', was not where the Stafford family's avian pets were kept, as they had none. The 'bird's room' was just a closet sized room, a bump out from the main thirty feet by thirty-ish-feet rectangular main-house structure, no more than six by eight feet, extending off to the right as you entered the living room, that room housing the family's only TV and thus, usually occupied (SRO) from after dinner until bedtime. The 'bird's room' did not have a door, thus, it not really being Walter's private 'lair' but it did have one small window. This window did not open, it was just a fixed pane of glass; that opening over-looking the family's eighteen feet round by four feet deep above ground pool, which at its nearest positioning to the house, was separated by no more than three or four feet from that fenestella. Walter often fantasized about opening that immovable aperture and diving head-first into the pool. A fantasy indeed, as the somewhat chubby Walter could, in no way, fit through that small portal. Nevertheless, we all do need our real or imaginary escape routes, regardless of the logic or clarity of mind that went into constructing such escapes.

Surrounding the pool, there was quite a bit of decking, fashioned with sweat, mostly Walter's dad, but the younger might have helped a bit, fetching dad a beer when needed and the younger taking a sip or two, thinking his dad never knew. The decking built from 2 x 4s, and 1 x 6s, perhaps, sanded, no splinters needed, and hastily stained. Beyond the pool, there existed a few potting sheds, hand-built with hewn stone foundations, one composed to approximate a small greenhouse, built by long and recently dead maternal-side antecedents and slowly being reclaimed by mother earth. This imitation greenhouse was somewhat newer, built, perhaps, twenty or so years in the past, all these structures being built by the Plaro, originally Palauro, side of the family, Austrian descent but strongly identifying as Italians, as the maternal side of this family also having roots in northern and western Italy.

These decaying Italian buildings no longer had a function but in the past were put to very good use, providing a home to grow a variety of vegetables destined for the Plaro family consumption throughout the year.

Especially important were these maturing life verde in the spring, when an array of seedings would be planted, allowed to mature for perhaps eight to twelve weeks and then transplanted; a move of about one hundred yards or so to the south and become part of the formidable garden, which the entire Plaro family, several generations in fact, nurtured, for personal use only, for a many few years.

While actively growing, the fruits of the Plaro family labors would oft disappear before reaching the kitchen, consumed right off the vine, usually with a bit of salt and dirt as well, both enhancing the flavors. A tasty, but now sadly disappearing pleasure for most. Some of those vegetables that survived would be preserved, processed in a sundry of ways, single items and combinations thereof; thus, supplying the family with a variety of treats to last throughout the harsh, vegetable-free New England winters. These condiments and garnishes, perhaps a few serving as an *amuse-bouche*, would accompany some finely prepared meat dish; along with some type of 'starch' and voila, a feast for all. Throughout Walter's Little League years, the family did still keep a garden, but the newer gardens were not grown from seeds. Some plants were purchased and sowed after the last frost, often it wasn't quite the last and that could be a problem, which could come unusually late in this western Massachusetts town.

Beyond these putrefying structures was nothingness; a wild mostly unexperienced and virgin forest, full of small creatures, scary stories, hastily started but then aborted ventures, at times with Walter's sister, and on fewer occasions friends, but more often than not, Walter going solo, embarking on a journey, starting a quest or a crusade, a *jihad* perhaps, all these fictional adventures usually taking place within, the largely under-stimulated, and overly-internalized consciousness that was Walter; thus, the forest remained largely unexplored as it was far too dark and untamed to venture very far into.

In the very small 'bird's room', there existed a desk, Walter spent hours at this desk doing 'stuff', typically reading but also 'working on his coin collection or his stamp collection or sorting his baseball cards into teams, just 'stuff.'' The desk was built into the wall that was to the right of the window. His chair was simply a spare dining room chair; removed and put back into use at the dining room table when needed. The chair was dark stained pine, some non-descript woven, mass-produced, upholstery fabric, a geometric pattern of some kind, covering, both, the vertical and horizontal seating and reclining surfaces, Walter's version of the Herman Miller chair. A gooseneck reading lamp, with a low wattage, eye-straining and as inexpensive as possible, GE or knockoff lightbulb, provided the lighting for this small room. And it being called the 'bird's room' since occupying pretty much every vertical surface, most of the desktop and whatever space was available on the several shelves, simply made, angle iron, and 1 x 8 x 48 inches of common pine, most of the space used to host Walter's fairly extensive collection of used books, but occupying the free space were many fine example of the skills of the local taxidermist(s), mostly birds, pheasants, partridges, and perhaps a few squirrels, it being a small room. Uncle Al, Walter's mom's younger brother, residing with the family in this past-time as he was unemployed then, and in fact for whatever time frame from zero to infinity you so happen to choose, then not quite forty, a Korean War vet, details of his adventures in that war, non-war, conflict, more speculated upon than really known, was an avid hunter and he would barter with these local businessmen trading his latest conquest, a nice word for kill, these kills providing, perhaps, venison from deer or an assortment of other edible meats and the taxidermists doing what they do, immortalizing these slain creatures into trophies that Al would bring home to adorn the 'bird's room', or perhaps, engage in a second barter, if the creature was too big for the very small 'bird's room', trading a well-mounted deer's head for other consideration.

Al was an expert huntsman and the title was far less abhorrent back then, in fact, not abhorrent at all, and during that past time, young Walter had no moral judgments regarding the *abstraction* of hunting. Now, of course, if one of the many deer, which roam the older younger Walter's front meadow, starts munching on his prized lilies or the omni present Black-Eyed Susan's, which he has quite a fondness for, Walter will race out the front door, nowadays he is pretty much always at home having eschewed people and society in general, screaming and waving his arms in a very convincing imitation or mimicry of a mad-man, running directly at the deer if he is so inclined, having to wade through three or four feet high tick invested meadow grass or wild-flowers, aka over-priced weeds, in an attempt to scare those domesticized creatures who will simply stare back at him dumbly, expertly mimicking that vacant expression we see in so many of the offspring of the aristocrats who occupy(ied) and rule(d) most of the upper echelon Fairfield County communities; you can alternatively imagine the look, head titled in confusion, of an over-bred Labrador as well, the quintessential dog of Fairfield County.[5] If particularly stressed, for any of a

---

[5] Regression towards the mean provides an explanation for how the progeny, these filial accessories of the effulgent, the auroral, the privileged, the elite, the gentry, those pillars of industry and society who carved out Fairfield County, mostly Greenwich, Darien, and New Canaan, into what once was a bastion of wealth, isolation, protectionism, and such, but has been rapidly vaporizing under the tutelage of Governor Malloy (now former Govenor) and other Demoncrats; excuse me here, typo, Democrats, perhaps, not a typo, have morphed into mindless, tenantless, caricatures of their forebearers, simply being, often not doing and when doing, doing in confusion, just as the

number of reasons and Walter is always stressed, Walter has said a number of times; paraphrasing a line from a favorite author 'I am permanently stressed and outraged at the inability of our government, collective society, and we, the people, individually to live up even to the lowest standards of fairness, compassion, respectability, pretty much anything at all' however, if unnerved, as he always is, on occasion, too frequently, in fact, Walter will take out his Vokey 56° wedge, the only golf club remaining ex-basement, since his having given up golf for the second and arguably the last time, grab a new $4; a pop, Titleist, proV1 golf ball, a dozen being the yearly Christmas or birthday gift from his investment people, a number of dozens gathering garage dust, as they, the investment people, not knowing he has given up golf, drop the ball on a suitable surface, that surface ideally being somewhat forgiving to soften the impact of the club hitting such surface, but not an absolute requirement since we have often seen, and this is true, only if you watch golf on TV, a professional golfer hitting a ball off a paved, asphalt usually, cart path, with no untoward consequences, except, perhaps, to the club, which will be gratefully replaced by that particular professional golfer's sponsor at the end of the round, improper to do so during the round and incurring a penalty perhaps a DQ and attempt to scare the deer away by hitting the ball at or near the deer, if you are confused Walter *not* the professional golfer is trying to scare the deer.

---

aforementioned head titled in confusion Labrador! And, for the record, I am a Democrat but sometimes…

Now, let's digress a bit into the realm of evolution, seems straightforward, right? Evolution is an interesting science, although many of the disingenuous, let's be frank here and state for the record my use of disingenuous was actually a polite euphemism, the set I am actually referring to includes mostly the fanatically religious, let's throw in a few southern Republican senators and congressmen and idiots as well, perhaps, these last several groupings are a redundancy, believe evolution to be more or less witchcraft and not science at all, and these confused people deny it having any role whatsoever in, *uh*…evolution.

Well, one of my observations is, it, evolution, comes into play more often than one would think in everyday life. Deer were never threatened, chased, dismembered nor consumed by flying golf balls; therefore, they have no fear of a golf ball, that fear has not been evolved, racing towards them at perhaps fifty miles per hour. A small white ball as a predator is not hardwired into their brain's fight-or-flight, for deer flight only, response; probably true for pretty much any creature at all, except perhaps a green's keeper. So, unless the ball was heading directly towards the head of the deer, in such case they might confuse the golf ball with perhaps a gigantic white deer fly and to be avoided, it was of no concern, thus, in their tiny brain, mission control issues the 'let's keep on munching' directive. To all this deer psychology, add the fact that it is almost impossible to hit a deer with a wedge when the deer is only thirty or forty yards from you. A wedge is designed to hit high and land soft, a club you use to hit your ball onto the green at a pre-determined point, hopefully, near the hole, and stop immediately, actually, spin back if you are in possession of such advanced skills, Walter not so. So, to hit that offending deer with the wedge, it, being only thirty or so yards away, you would have to close down the face of the club, i.e. reduce the angle of impact, and hit a punch shot, i.e. terminate your follow through, and keep the ball low, not what the club is designed for. A difficult shot for a tiger, no, not that tiger, the Tiger, but perhaps, not that difficult for Mr. W, he can pull off shots of seeming impossibility, but Walter, very un-Tiger-like Walter, certainly not a shot Walter has ever successfully executed. Especially true, since on these occasions, it is quite probable that Walter did not go through a structured pre-shot routine, now, a necessary element to hit the perfect golf shot and perhaps, capture of a few more seconds of valuable prime-time TV, since it was likely prior to spotting this marauding creature Walter was in his house or gym, engaged in some meaningless activity, when upon spotting the deer, ran off to the garage, fetched his Vokey wedge, ran somewhere else to find a golf ball, the dust collecting Pro V 1's, then relocating the three, Walter the ball and the wedge, to within striking proximity of the deer, dropped the ball onto whatever surface was available, giving no thought as to the consequences to the club or to Walter's wrist of hitting that $4 golf-ball at the offending deer off a surface with no give. The shot would be made, it would be close, but of no concern to the deer. After the shot, Walter would grasp his wrist in pain, for the one hundred and seventh time, just a guess at the number, but ultimately, the deer would continue to munch; and so what, it was a big field with lots of flowers! Walter accepting defeat, clutching his injured wrist, would head back towards the kitchen and apply one of his many icepacks, these icepacks, now, becoming a more essential element of life for Walter's wrists both left and right and he would not consider escalating this deer man conflict to protect his precious flowers. Correction, he does often *consider* escalation, mostly in his mind, but at times, going so far as to being only a click away from purchasing from Amazon that Walther PPQ pellet gun a doppelganger of the real Walther PPK, the gun Adolf Hitler allegedly used, in a sense, to transmogrify his both, physical and earthly form, and let's not forget that the Walther PPK was James Bond's gun of choice, having been advised of the superiority of this weapon by Dr. No. But thankfully, no, there are no guns of any sort in Walter's shopping cart!

Now, let's go back to the original Al digression. In this past time, Al and on occasions, an older younger Walter, (in this Al digression, we are referencing a Walter when he was thirteen or fourteen not nine, the age he was when this supposed baseball discourse began, and which seems to be melting into the distant past) would roust themselves out of bed early in the pre-dawn hours, in the burgeoning fall and prepare for that ageless male bonding experience, the first day of hunting season. Plans were made well in advance by Al, of course, the date upon which hunting season would commence was well publicized. Of course, local papers carried such announcements but if you ventured into any coffee shop, variety store, smoke's shop, or 'package' store, a not quite unique term for liquor store in this past time and place, likely an animated conversation or many would be ongoing as to the particulars of the first day of the season. If opening day happened to fall on a week-day, Mrs. Stafford would not allow Walter to miss school; therefore, on those occasions, Walter's first day of the hunt would be Saturday, but that wasn't important, there was plenty game to be had.

Water's bedroom was on the second floor of the tiny Stafford family house, even with three tiny bedrooms on the second floor, the house was barely over one thousand square feet. A prominent feature of Walter's bedroom was a three or four-inch diameter metal pipe, covered with perhaps twenty layers of lead-based paint, so it was hardly recognizable as metal anymore, running from the basement up through the room in the interior of the bedroom, located just behind the headboard of Walter's bed and between the east most wall of the room, terminating somewhere above the roofline in the attic crawlspace of Walter's bedroom. Walter always thought this intrusive structure was just a water pipe[6] but being there were no second-floor bathrooms, clearly not the case. It was likely an exhaust, originating in the basement of the house a part of some long ago removed heating device, designed to burn wood or coal, and needing sufficient venting as not to create toxic plumes of gas and suffocate the entire family residing therein. The house was built in the late 1890s, so there were seventy or so years, during which structural modifications could have obfuscated the original intent of this aged metal-pipe, completely hiding its original purpose.

However, on Saturday mornings, this pipe of questionable provenance became an alarm clock, Al, in the

---

[6] We are referring to a plumbing structure, carrying water. Further on in this narrative, in Walter's college years, water pipe will take on a whole new meaning.

kitchen, rapping gently on the pipe, in an attempt to roust the Younger, with one of his many pipes; Al smoked pipes, cigars, cigarettes, hemp, meadow grass, pretty much anything combustible; the house was small and loud noises could have disturbed the entire household; but Al was discreet, rapping loudly enough only to awaken Walter, and he, Walter, quickly throwing on the appropriate hunting garb, it wasn't really hunting garb, just his every day wear, simply jeans and a sweatshirt, all hand me downs, would spring out of bed, throw on his clothes and rush down to meet Al in the kitchen.

They would coffee up, brewed Maxwell House from a can, it was called a percolator, the coffeemaker, not the can, strong and bitter; then brewing temperatures were much higher than they should have been to make proper coffee, probably more than 195°F, which is arguably considered to be the optimal brewing temperature. But this was 1960s coffee, no Starbucks, no gourmet coffee, what 'da fuck' was a Barista in 1960s rural *Americana*? It was coffee and it did the trick. Caffeine is an amazing drug. In the *further*, or if we simply change a single letter in the word further and change the *h* to a *u*, and drop an *r* and rearrange, the *future* adventures of Walter, we will learn about the diversity of drugs that played a subordinate role in Walter's, and let's use the aforementioned discussed word here, evolution. However, while Walter had short-lived affairs with many different chemistries, his one true and long-lasting love was, Quaaludes, sorry, typo, caffeine! So, on these preternatural Saturday mornings, of which, there were probably only a few but memory being a liquid and adapting it's form to the vessel it occupies, in Walter's mind, at least, there were many, far too many, Al and Walter would coffee up, grab their gear, which included an assortment of single shot and semi-automatic rifles, no fully-automatic weapons back then, head off into the country, even though, in actuality, you were living in the country, park your car on a deserted dead-end gravel or dirt road, tromp through the bramble and somewhat dense forests of western Massachusetts, lots of ferns, moss, and assorted bushes with 'prickers', and through some, somehow acquired or perhaps, evolutionarily ingrained skills, determine where a deer was or would be, track the aforementioned deer, stealth-fully position yourself within fifty or so yards of that deer and fire at great speed, up to 2,500 feet per second, a lead projectile into that once beautiful living creature. Al would, of course, be the shooter, while Walter took extensive target practice, he never once shot or shot at a living creature. If the first lead projectile was off target and simply struck an injurious wound, when the poor creature, mortally injured, was writhing and agonizing on the earthly forest, beginning its transcendental journey of becoming one with its destined to be final and forever home, uncle Al, perhaps now residing in the ninth level of Dante's Hell, no probably the seventh, yes, it definitely is the seventh, which is violence. Strange that the ninth level is fraud, is fraud worse than violence, not today for sure, however, Dante was from many centuries past and I guess a lot of deference was given to Judas, would put the poor creature out of its misery; a euphemism, perhaps, so much debate possible, with a second projectile. If the gentle creature was substantially adorned, antlers, the male deer were rated with a point system as to the abundance of their horn, consideration as to where the next shot, the lethal shot was to be placed was paramount, so as not to interfere with what might become a treasured wall display for Al or one of his conspirators, by the way there were no deer trophies in the 'bird's room'; too small, the room that is, not the trophies.

What transpired after the kill shot was butchery itself, literally and figuratively, and simply in the sense of preparing and butchering the animal, and taking usable parts of this former creature, those parts, which allowed that animal to serve a second purpose after its murder, that purpose to provide food and perhaps, a trophy as well. Al with Walter's distracted assistance, Walter developed a rich fantasy life, often to block out hideous moments like these, would drag or carry the bloodied, former animal back to the car, secure it to the front bumper or roof of the vehicle, proudly, only Al, drive home, and there, back at the Stafford family residence, Al would, like a returning hero from Troy, Homer's Troy not Troy, NY, which by the way, would be the home of the older younger Walter's college adventures and adventures might be too strong a word, but more later, broadcast his account of the battle won, the remarkable events of the day. He pacing back and forth, smoking his pipe, with vigorous animation, using the pipe as a laser pointer and at times, when appropriate his weapon, wherein, he would describe in minutia, the so important details of the track and the kill; this lasting likely minutes, but seemingly hours, he, pacing and gesticulating, with the intensity of an addict or more appropriately a recreational drug user should be referenced, perhaps, wherein, effects can be even more pronounced; regardless, Al's diatribe was his drug; he began to feel the rush of endorphins, the release of neurotropic factors, he experienced a runner's high, without covering more than thirty feet, the longest axis of the Stafford household; his allocution released endogenous cannabinoids, a variety of naturally produced stimulants coursing through his circulatory system, as he regaled the family with the adventure, repeating the heroic parts, establishing his position in the social order, that was the event most momentous. And nearby, Walter quietly and distractedly listening or trying, not to perhaps, and more likely the case, in the 'bird's room', surrounded by former living creatures, preserved not in perpetuity but for at least a reasonable number of years, preserved and remembered, until they were not, but undoubtedly, this period lasting more years than the time they survived in the quite dangerous forests adjacent to New Apley.

Walter did not need nor want to hear this seminar 'Murder most foul' he was there, after all, but he did hear it, since while in the 'bird's room', he was no more than a mere few feet away from the speaker's platform, as the entire first floor was less than eight hundred feet square. Walter, in the room alone, half listening, while reading, perhaps, Dante, Shakespeare, or some other escapist collection; these collections, simply being words transcribed onto pieces of paper, and those pages being bound together with leather and glue, somewhat ironic, both, the leather and glue actually products derived from slaughtered animals, mostly cows bred and slaughtered for meat but the skin and underlying tissue providing a secondary usefulness, words leaping from the paper into Walter's mind, many missing bouncing in all directions, a Feynman approach the words adopted, trying to take every possible path before finding a room inside, what the words were, not really mattering, just some story to take Walter somewhere, somewhere beyond the then and there.

# Part 2

## Bunsen, Bowling, and Golf

The elder Walter considered having another drink before informing the family as to the results of that organizational Little League meeting, and after some less than deep reflection, decided in the affirmative. Addressing the family was something the Elder cared not to do, ever, whether the reason be trivial or of major import. He was not an actor, he hated taking the stage, whether being alone or in a group, he was in fact, quite shy and reserved. A drink, another drink, although he had a quite few at the club, would be necessary to get him through, this seemingly to others, nothing of an event, a drink always seemed to help. He poured himself a short drink, two fingers, but he did have really fat fingers, Gordon's gin with rocks, no water, and was now ready to begin his oration. With drink in hand, and now completely composed, Walter, the Elder, informed younger Walter and the collected family, that he, the Elder would be coaching a team in the league and younger Walter would be on the team. Dad, along with Bunsen Supernatant, a family friend, about fifteen years younger than the elder Walter and a majority owner and manager of the soon to be opened local bowling establishment Mt. Fetlock Bowl, would be sharing the coaching duties. Bunsen, like the elder Walter, was also a former local high school multi-sport athlete and in the real sports; football, basketball, and baseball. Bunsen's son was not on the team, as he was a year or two younger than the younger Walter and was not eligible to play. It was a rarity for an adult male to volunteer to coach Little League without an eligible son, it just didn't happen, in fact, why should it, what's the upside to spending undue amounts of time with a bunch of sniveling nine to twelve year old's, throwing hours of batting practice which will undeniably result in future shoulder, wrist, or elbow arthritis, if at least one of the sniffling brats isn't a blood relative. Today, one might suspect an ulterior motive, such that the son-less coach might be a pedophile, but this was not the case in those carefree and pedophile-free 1960s.

The Stafford's and Supernatants were close friends, all four, moms and dads; no concealed motives, no mutual financial interests, no secondary business motives, just friends, it happens or happened! Bunsen, his wife, and the Stafford's would often get together, usually on a Sunday early evening, a down time in the bowling world, for a well-deserved celebration at the end of a long work week; far longer, in real hours, and physically far more taxing for Mr. Stafford, in part to recap the not so exciting, usually just irksome, events of the week, but mostly to drink themselves into a short-lived stupor, that stupor being the only way to forget the many stressful and unsolvable problems of the week past and of course, those same problems waiting to rise up again, not Phoenix-like, very real and not symbolic, only more magnified on the following Monday. These important discussions would begin only after a well-prepared meal, beer, wine, and hard booze accompanying all the courses, the Stafford's usually preparing something classically Italian; pasta and some sort of meat, manicotti stuffed with a mixture of pork, veal and beef was a favorite. The Supernatants, Bunsen, but not his wife, having an aboriginal Alaskan heritage would have a running joke, wherein, when queried about his heritage he would respond "You pick," the questioning party thinking this was a joke and Bunsen simply being evasive; however, Bunsen's joke was that he was poorly pronouncing his actual heritage, he being more or less a 50% member of the Yupik, pronounced 'Ju'-peek', the indigenous Alaskan people, but in his version, spoken as 'you pick.' Thus, pulling from Bunsen's youthful traditions, the Supernatant's would usually prepare a simple fish dish, (thankfully nothing exotic neither whale blubber nor seal meat was available in New Apley in these times as these were often the meal of choice for certain Yupik tribes. Other tribes seemed to subsist on caribou and berries, however all seemed to adhere to the now fashionable *paleo* diet). Often, the Supernatant's would simply grill some North Atlantic Salmon, without any flare, quite healthy, however, something the Stafford foursome found quite dull. In spite of the quite massive alcohol consumption, mostly by the men, Bunsen and elder Walter, always recovered sufficiently to safely drive the family back to the home court. The families lived at least ten miles apart, the Supernatants actually living outside the city limits, and these ten miles were considered quite a distance to travel for any social engagement in this past time and place. These times back then, only sixty years or so in the past, nonetheless, were quite different, far simpler than today. Big cars, empty roads, no DUI checkpoints, and very few incidents, dangerous, injurious, or whatever; why, I cannot hazard a guess, however, life seemed to be safer, simpler, and more honest and secure back then.

These weekly celebrations of life were home and away events; sometimes, the Supernatant's hosted, other times, the Stafford's. Younger Walter more vividly recalls the away events, as it wasn't very often he had the opportunity to stray away from the homestead for any social gathering or pretty much for anything at all.

The Stafford family residence was nothing to speak of; it provided a roof over the head of family members. While Bunsen was somewhat successful, the family home did not entirely reflect his financial status, but it certainly was a world apart from the Stafford's Whitway Street home.

It was a simple one-story ranch, with three bedrooms off to the side. The kitchen had modern appliances, including a dishwasher, something alien to the Stafford's, and there was even a laundry room. Not a basement, cellar actually, there is a difference believe me, and in the Stafford's household it was a cellar and there was a washer and dryer very inconveniently located in such. The Younger recalls, it was quite a scary trip if mom requested the Younger to assist in the cleaning of the family clothes, poor lighting, a stairwell meeting perhaps, a building code from William the Great's time, and no telling what form of flora or fauna, from a large spider to a small rodent, would be encountered in simply retrieving the freshly laundered family finery, but in the Supernatant's home, there was a room actually designed for the efficient cleaning and organization of family sundries.

The kitchen opened out onto a quite large family room, designed to be the center of life. A somewhat oversized for the time, perhaps, twenty-five inch TV, a reel-to-reel tape deck with obscenely large and likely poor quality stereophonic speakers occupied two of the four walls, and there, on the coffee table, in the exact center of the room, and I do mean exact, Bunsen, after all, was by training an engineer, sat his prized possession and likely the centerpiece of this evening's drama and most evenings in fact, the chessboard.

Bunsen and the younger Walter spent a good portion of the evening playing chess in this family room. Bunsen was a fine player and introduced Walter to the game. Bunsen, as did the Younger, started playing chess as a child, but not in the long twenty hour plus sun-less winter days of his family's Alaskan home; no, Bunsen, never saw his tribal home, having been born and spending his entire life up to this point in time in the New Apley universe. After dinner, sometimes before, Bunsen would set up the chess board, an elaborately crafted object *d'art* and something you would not expect to see in a town, the ilk of New Apley. All the pieces were hand carved, Bunsen claimed the set, a treasure and in his keeps since a child, was created by a famous, although the identity unknown or long forgotten, Inuit artisan; each piece was meticulously carved from walrus tusks, the black pieces dyed, according to Bunsen with whale's blood, however, this was believed by all to be hyperbole. Each individual piece looked like a work in progress, rough, little fine detail, almost a weathered type of look. The pawns appeared to be siblings but each was slightly different, they were unique. The bishops seemed to be some sort of fish, perhaps, a primordial seal and the other pieces each bore, both a distinct tribal and piscine element. The board itself was a rough-hewn leather from seal's skin. The white squares were not white, but were only slightly lighter than the darker squares and these seemed to be the seal's natural color, thirty-two of each, painstakingly hand-stitched together with a synthetic composite fishing line; the skin's normal water protective sheen was missing, presumably lost in the processing. This patched together eight-by-eight seal's skin matrix was mounted upon a quite heavy piece of wood, unknown origin, lending support and integrity. Younger Walter recalls that this unique chessboard was quite heavy, weighing more than sixteen pounds, the weight of the heaviest bowling ball, but we all know how time, age, and memories can change facts, so who knows and who cares what the real weight was. Although Bunsen was the far better player, younger Walter often won. The younger acknowledges that some of the victories came after Bunsen was well beyond the 0.08% blood alcohol limit, this limit being the gold standard for defining sobriety, at least for the purpose of driving a motor vehicle, chess, who knows, thus, Bunsen was playing under the influence, not a punishable crime back in the 1960s at least for chess[7]. Walter, however, believes Bunsen tanked

---

[7] It turns out the blood alcohol content for determining intoxication was not 0.08% in these past times, that gold standard was not established until the early 2000s. In 1938 based upon drunk driving fatality statistics the American Medical Association recommended a level of 0.15%, WOW that's almost double today's standard and that level equates to about eight or ten drinks

quite a few of those weekly matches, some, perhaps many, that in fact he played sober, as it was likely Bunsen realized young Walter needed these little, meaningless victories, these positive affirmations, just something, something real and tangible, to ward off the omnipresent and growing exponentially, internal demons of self-deprecation. As time passed, these matches became less frequent, the Stafford-Supernatant bond was being drawn asunder by external forces from known and unknown directions, however, on those occasions, when these fondly remembered rituals of adolescence were repeated, younger Walter was, with no help needed, routinely beating Bunsen. Chess was a meaningless game, a mental exercise, an endeavor that was harmonious with and aligned very nicely with the probing and over-analytical structure of young Walter's internally directed mind and his somewhat obsessive desire to stay inside that mind. Why venture forth into the real world when safety and a completely predicted future existed, as Walter hid in elaborately created rooms, not the 'bird's room', but safe and secure havens, rooms that looked like the ones he saw on the 'Soaps', which his mom would watch every day and these never to be experienced rooms, other than in his mind, away and isolated from the harsh

---

over a two- to four-hour period, another WOW needed here. In fact in the 1960s drunk driving was considered a way of life, perhaps a rite of passage; there was little enforcement, a slap on the wrist, perhaps a slap on the back in fact, "Dammit Jimmie's becoming a man!" America is slowly changing for the better, rejecting those *Wild West* freedoms, freedoms endangering the good of the many, of course except for guns!

realities of the outside, the real world. This mindly mansion of the Younger, permitting no visitors, allowed for the constant revision of games lost, replaying over and over until won. As with many things, Walter wasn't a prodigy, and would not have a future in chess, other than his high school chess club, he was simply quite good.

Bunsen was an engineer by trade, having worked at Craig Electric in the center of downtown New Apley and about four hundred yards from the elder Walter's business Lakeside Auto Body[8].

---

[8] During these Little League years, Walter's Dad, Walter the Elder, was about fifty years old but he was an old fifty, physically at least, having worked after being discharged from the army in several different auto body shops. The last shop he would work in for more than twenty years, he was actually a co-owner of, Lakeside Auto Body, located in New Apley on River Street, just a few blocks from where he was born and spent most of his life. There, he worked alongside his partner, Peter, the two of them pounding out dents, filling in those dents with compounding material, sanding with increasingly fine grades of sand paper, first by machine, next an orbital sander operating on 120 volts, and then by hand, first using a buffing compound and finally, as the ultimate step in this laborious process, using with considerable skill, fine steel wool, rubbing the metal and compounding fill in circular motions until those repaired patches were flawlessly smooth, and indistinguishable from the neighboring factory finished surfaces, and although masked, he and his partner both breathing in the microscopic fiberglass dust particles, not asbestos but from a pharmacological perspective not all that different, then spraying aerosolized paint onto those smoothly sanded surfaces, breathing in more miniscule solid particles of this not quite gaseous paint and after that, at the end of the day, cleaning up,

hands, arms, and face, by dipping a cotton rag into a 55-gallon drum of benzene, next taking that benzene saturated rag and vigorously rubbing all skin surfaces until free of paint, new and old, and the fiberglass-based compounding material, and when visually clean, another wipe with benzene just to be sure. Hands, faces, and arms were often tender and red after this quotidian ritual, in part from the toxic benzene but also from the abrasive and exfoliating effect of forcefully rubbing a rag, likely having accumulated several days' worth of fiberglass compounding materials, onto the skin's tender surface. Your 1960s auto-body shop 'Buff Puff.' Thus, the elder Walter, suffering from these not so healthy daily duties, from a biological perspective was a really old fifty; please note, however, the daily exfoliation detailed above did keep both his hands and face surprisingly young looking.

There was a small three inch or so circular opening, not quite in the center of the drum top and this could be used to insert a pump or hose to dispense the benzene, but not the case for this drum. On those drums used at the body shop, the entire top would be removed. It, the top, was held in place with a metal gasket. This gasket, more or less, a circular semi-circle, think of a hula hoop sliced in half along the horizontal circumference, would be placed around at the top of the drum covering the edges of both, the separate drum top and the upper or top rim of the drum. There was a lever or ratchet on the gasket and when the gasket was firmly in place, the lever would be folded back upon itself one hundred and eighty degrees, the process making a tight seal between the top and sides, so no liquid could escape. The removal of the top was necessary as not just hands or rags, but small auto parts as well were dipped into the benzene. Back in 1969, benzene was simply an industrial grade solvent used to clean away the dirt of the day. Over the years, information concerning the toxic and carcinogenic effects of benzene accumulated, actually, its toxicity was identified as early as 1928, and at some point, the early 1970s, it was deemed by the powers to be, the FDA, OSHA, etc. that this material was unsafe, that it was killing people, and it should not be used in pure form and only used under controlled conditions and only when other options were not available. As often said 'timing is everything.'

As with most sons, at some point, in time, that son wants to do what his dad does, join him on the job. Younger Walter never seriously entertained the idea of following his dad into the automotive business, re-inventing himself as Walter Ace Body-Guy 2.0, but regardless of logic and reason, there appears to exist some biological pull or imperative for a son to emulate his dad and follow in his steps, even though those steps might be heading towards parts unknown and unwanted, perhaps, like lemmings and onto the precipice we must go, but even thinking of taking such a path, trying to breathe some life into a flailing and failing business and keep it afloat, having no skills or natural talent in the area of car repair, would have been absurd. Luckily for younger Walter, Walter the Elder, was adamantly set against this footstep following, he wanted and expected a better life for his children, that was his *raison d'etre*. However, the Younger did spend a considerable number of days in the shop during that period of time between high school graduation and off to college, about three months, and during those days, Walter, the Younger, dipped assorted body parts, auto and self into the benzene, and at the end of one of those days, the 55-gallon drum of benzene being contaminated from the rag dipping and the necessary insertion of assorted car parts for cleaning, the benzene became too dirty to use and since a new 55-gallon drum had just arrived, Walter, the Elder, and the Younger, would cap the old drum and with some care, as it did weigh as much as three hundred pounds attributable to a 0.876 specific gravity of benzene and loss of perhaps thirty gallons through use, tilt the drum slightly and roll it, as in a drunkards walk. If you have ever rolled, and rolled is clearly the wrong word, a 55-gallon drum, you will immediately grasp the visual I'm trying to draw. It really isn't rolling in the sense of tipping the drum on its long side and actually rolling. You tilt the drum, perhaps ten to fifteen degrees off vertical and roll the drum along the bottom rim always taking a serpentine path. Elder, fifty-ish-year-old Walter and younger, likely eighteen-year-old Walter, awkwardly rolled that 55-gallon drum to the back of the shop, removed the top, and cautiously tipped the drum over, allowing it to fall unhindered to the ground on its vertical side; some splash back to be avoided, however, this process efficiently emptied the drum and allowed the gentle earth to graciously accept the then not yet determined to be quite toxic and carcinogenic benzene into her/his/itself at the anterior exterior of the shop, that shop being Lakeside Auto Body. What became of the drum itself is a mystery.

I'm not sure how many times this actually happened or even if this happened at all, and all this is perhaps a created false memory; this recollection is most unlikely to be a false memory, however, the author is simply posing this possibility to avoid any legal repercussions, which although implausible, are possible, since in today's world, the backwards reach of class action suits and spurious accusations usually against celebrities or the super-rich seem to be becoming commonplace, however, if one happens to be staying in one the local B and B's, a night will actually set you back $500 or more, hard to believe, and close proximity to the non and never-existent Lakeside Auto Body, or dining in one of the local in vogue, hipster restaurants that now abound since the re-gentrification of New Apley and the surrounding area I would opt for bottled water. But repeating myself, that's just silly talking, because even if five or ten drums of benzene were dumped into the graciously receptive earthly maiden over twenty years, and that being almost fifty years ago, we would not be talking about

Being somewhat ahead of his time and eschewing the mantra of the sixties 'work hard until you die', Bunsen burned out, not really he simply quit, dropped out, no, just a change in career, quite common today, and invested his hard-earned money, he admitted it was actually pretty easy work, earned from a pretty prestigious engineering job, and that money being quite substantial for New Apley, into Mt. Fetlock Bowl, a thirty-six-lane establishment, with full bar and grill and pinball machines as well.

Words cannot adequately describe New Apley of the 1960s, this being the author's perspective only, but let's give it a go. Time changes everything, so the fifty plus years between then and now has destroyed probable comparisons, so even if you lived in that past time, unless you lived in a similar rural, lower socio-economic class American town, trying to imagine how life was in New Apley, is just a non-productive exercise. Nevertheless, some current examples might be appropriate, one being the current Albuquerque, New Mexico. I've been there, recently, for a Dermatology

---

another Love Canal or toxic cleanup site that we so often see in my favorite state of New Jersey. Given that New Apley typically gets fifty plus inches of snow per year, this vast amount of moisture absorbed into the accepting terra would purify the local aquifer and dilute any amount of the fifty-year-old benzene remaining, so as to be of no consequence. Additionally, Lakeside Auto-body closed in 1976, when younger Walter was twenty-five, his dad having a quite debilitating stroke. We do not know what became of Peter. Upon closure, there were no assets derived from this defunct, fictional business; therefore, it is unlikely a class action suit is in the works, even in the imagination of the most dedicated paranoid. Footnote ended!

Conference, why the convention chose Albuquerque I have no fucking idea as to why, perhaps, deeply discounted convention facilities and a block of cheap hotel rooms. This is likely the case as my recollection details that within the immediate confines of the Convention Center there existed more empty prime downtown building lots than buildings. There were very visible signs of rampant drug use and sale on street corners and remarkably high unemployment in spite of Obama/Trumpian economics; in fact, hotels near the surprisingly frequently booked Convention Center warn guests to travel in groups, make sure your cell phones are fully charged, only carry a single credit card and no cash, and have your affairs in order before you venture forth, if brave enough, into the downtown. Sorry, Albuquerque. Mis-quoting Dennis Miller, "Just my opinion, I may be wrong."

I'm rolling now, more descriptors are available. Let's imagine; pretty much any city subjected to a devastating Ebola virus epidemic, discovery of the plague, high levels of lead, mercury, or other toxins in the drinking water, and, *yes*, thinking of Flint Michigan here, the sudden revelation that nuclear waste was buried nearby or the simple fact that too many people, perhaps, slightly inbred, not cousin to cousin, no we are not invoking memories of 'Deliverance', simply a paucity of genetic diversity in part due to a lack of movement into and out of the community, where there are not enough jobs, culture, or anything of interest to do. I may be overstating, we have already established or hinted that the Younger, was, at times, somewhat delusional, but even if we are drawing a hyperbolic caricature of New Apley in the 1960s, this is likely a place you would not have chosen to grow up in.

Let's acknowledge, however, that time changes real and perceived facts, memories as well, and *yes*, let's throw on top of that I may have a virtual axe to grind, nevertheless, even with such considerations, New Apley was clearly subterranean, had not broken the surface with respect to almost anything regarding culture or entertainment. Thus, it was pretty obvious and a given, that any new venture brought to New Apley, promoting anything with any entertainment value whatsoever, would likely be an overwhelming success, a hurdle not too high to leap over. In New Apley, towards the end of that first year younger Walter started his Little League odyssey, Bunsen opened Mt. Fetlock Bowl and just over the state line in Pownal Vermont, Green Mountain Race Track, opened its doors to pretty much a year-round program of harness (Standardbred) and flat (Thoroughbred) racing. Both sports-based ventures became instant successes, each becoming social centers for the slightly spiritless residents of New Apley and the surrounds, but more importantly, both venues became a major part of young Walter's life, beginning coincidentally and concurrent with his start of Little League baseball and ending for Walter, at least one of these two ventures still exists today, when he headed off to college.

From the very first day Mt. Fetlock Bowl opened its doors the Stafford's and the Supernatant's became permanent residents of the lanes, the happy foursome bowling, drinking, smoking cigarettes, usually, but not always putting down those burning orange torches when it was their turn to roll that ebony sphere down the lanes, but most importantly, simply to ingurgitate the waters of socialization like a dry sponge. The elder Walter and Mrs. Stafford bowled in the Friday mixed doubles league, which was the place to be in New Apley for a couple on a Friday night. Bunsen and his wife could not join in, they would likely have been the Stafford's obvious bowling partners; however, as this was the busiest night of the week, both, Bunsen and his wife were busy minding the shop. Younger Walter was always there, he could have stayed home with the extended family, his sister often did, however, the Younger assisted Bunsen at the desk. Walter's job was to spray disinfectant, he dares not to think of the composition of this likely toxic material and the vast volume of gaseous material he inhaled, as this was the 1960s, there was no Prop 65, and environmental toxins and carcinogens were commonplace, however these were likely tame compared to benzene, into each pair of returned bowling shoes, special shoes being required in order not to mar or damage the fine oak surfaces of the approach area on the alleyways and as well as to provide a low friction sole in order for the bowler to glide to the foul line as he or she released their ebony orb.[9]

---

[9] Bowling balls were pretty much standard, black in the early 1960s, unlike today, wherein, the color variation is considerable and not just colors, psychedelic displays and marbleized effects, which rival the interiors of many circa 1970 college dorm rooms. In fact, today professional bowlers will often have two distinctly different colored bowling balls, one for the first roll, and the second to convert spares. Back in the sixties, it was all black,

Walter and his sister, Barbara, within the family and among close friends, Bobbie, was the *nom du choice*, spent plenty of after school free time at the lanes and there was an ample amount of this free time back in the 1960s. In this past time, a day-planner was not included in the essential back to school garb for the typical teen; moreover, the practice of over mothering, mother's scheduling every half hour of everyday from the moment the final bell rang until dinner time had not yet been adopted as common practice. Both young Staffords were participants and became league stars and one might go as far as to say local celebrities in the Saturday and Sunday morning junior bowling leagues.

In fact, it was not just afternoons and weekends that were spent at the lanes. Walter has vivid and fond memories of his dad, picking him up at the beginning of school lunchbreak, about 11:50 a.m. or so, at Fetlock Elementary School, he was likely in fourth or fifth grade at the time, probably both years, and subsequently, the two of them driving the less than a quarter mile from the school to the closed Mt. Fetlock lanes. The drive, taken numerous times was imprinted on the younger Walter's mind and surprisingly still remains there, we do often retain useless information that was once important; the drive started at the main entrance of the three-story rectangular brick structure that was Fetlock Elementary School. At the start of lunchbreak, the younger would quickly exit the building, jump into the passenger's side front, and elder Walter would slowly advance down a slight incline only about a hundred

---

except, perhaps, for a blue ball or other subtle variations used as ladies' bowling balls.

yards in length, passing the sports fields on the left, next make a quick right at the bottom of the slope, a quick left would follow, another left, then a right onto a small side road, and then another quick left into Mt. Fetlock Bowl's huge parking lot. Bunsen would be there, he was always there doing something, usually paperwork, but Bunsen was a hands-on guy and would pitch in and help wherever help was needed. Being a former engineer, he could take care of any repairs, whether they be problems on the lanes or the pin setting machines, the pinball machines, heating and cooling, electrical issues, pretty much anything at all. The arrival of the two Walter's would give Bunsen cause to fire up the grill and cook a burger (or two) for Dad, Bunsen and himself. The adults would treat themselves to an early happy hour, perhaps a beer and on good days several, and the fat younger Walter would have several fully sugared real Cokes.

The exquisite taste of a burger from ones childhood (and perhaps it's only a burger memory and not the taste of the burger itself) cannot be remotely matched today, even by the $30-$50 Kobe beef burgers from the Hyogo Prefecture, those burgers you will likely find at the many privileged and overpriced restaurants of today. No, a burger back then in the 1960s was just a burger; it was just a slab of meat, obtained from ordinary cows. This memory burger, that the Younger and Elder shared, was likely about four ounces; a square or a rectangle, stamped out by some fabricated and hand operated piece of machinery, unlikely a hand formed circular patty, nothing special about the meat, not advertised as free range or organic, how silly to think of that as being of any importance, but there was a good chance that it was both free range, and organic, not genetically tinkered with or from Japan, there was no genetic tinkering back in the 1960s, actually there might have been but we, we being the lay public, didn't know about such. It was a local product and was harvested from happy cows, at least, for a short time, grazing naturally on grass. There is no doubt this memory burger was not lean, but no nutritional disclosures were required, so no one could tell or care about the fat content; undoubtedly, it had a very high fat content, possibly 30%, and distinctive marbling, which is the essence of a good burger. Preparation was nothing special, it was simply flung onto a hot, likely not too clean, flat piece of stainless, just a grill, residual meat grease, undeniably lubricating that surface, flipped and tossed, onto a white bread bun, also grilled, only after having been generously buttered on each side. Next came the accoutrements, a slice or two of bread and butter pickle, maybe, a slice of yellow not so over-processed cheese, and standard fare Del Monte's ketchup. The burger was clearly good, but for sure, the memory of its taste, even to this very day, is far better.[10]

---

[10] We all recognize that the odors and tastes of childhood stand out and occupy a place of enshrinement in our psyche when compared to our more current culinary experiences. Are these differences simply the result of time warping our impressions? Was the food actually better in these past times? Are we not so jaded that even a wonderful food experience of today seems tame? Or does physiological aging affect our ability to discriminate and enjoy? Many questions and yes, in varying degrees to all of these is the (my) answer! Numerous studies have shown age only modestly influences taste and those changes are pretty much directly related to changes in our sense of smell. It is quite clear

During these, Walter, Walter, and Bunsen moments existing in their own private world, conversation was sparse and pretty simple. Bunsen and Dad doing most of the talking, probably the topics trite and unimportant, perhaps, the universal weather discussion, complaining about work, the government, taxes, family, and life in general. If any important discussions were had, it was after younger Walter left the threesome, after which time, the two adults could enjoy some private, 1960s adult male time, whatever that means, younger Walter certainly didn't and its arguable he still has no idea as to the meaning of such. Younger Walter, during these times, was pretty much silent, inside his own head, no external stimuli permitted, and unless directly queried about something, he was content, simply concentrating on his burger. When the meal was over, on a good day, luck intervened, it was actually 'Lucky Phil' who intervened, that was his nickname. The luck had to do with some lost story concerning WWII, and the simple fact that Phil had survived was indeed the lucky aspect of the story. Lucky Phil was the lane's keeper, sort of the bowling alley equivalent to the green's keeper, and on occasion, Lucky Phil would turn on one of the lanes and bowl a game or two with younger Walter.[11]Digression terminated!

---

our memory of ancient tastings has an equally important impact as do changes in our sensorial talents.

[11] The younger Walter became quite an accomplished junior bowler, although, if queried, he would usually deny having any real talent for the game, his reasoning being, "I spent a lot of time at the lanes; there were only a few things you could do there; you could eat, disinfect bowling shoes, or bowl. I spent quite a bit of time doing each and became competent!"

Walter participated for a number of years in the junior bowling league at Mt. Fetlock Bowl every Saturday morning, sometime, Sunday mornings as well, in both individual and team competitions and in local tournaments and therein, honing his skills.

Younger Walter, in fact, in his twelfth year of being, 1963, competed in and won the Massachusetts State Junior Bowling Championship in the twelve-year old division. This event was held in Framingham, Massachusetts about a two hour plus drive from New Apley. Framingham was a Boston suburb, not a real suburb back in 1963, not a lot of commuters, just a bit too far to drive, when there were plenty of good paying local jobs to satisfy the workforce, but in spite of being a decidedly working-class, non-commuter town, it was imparted a degree of sophistication, compared to New Apley at least, this afforded by its proximity to the shining star of the Bay State, Boston. Walter was twelve at the time, in his third and last year of Little League and three years ahead in Newtonian time, of the main events of this baseball narrative. With just a smidge of foreshadowing, we will acknowledge that as a twelve-year-old bowler, Walter had made significant progress with respect to his 'disability', just a plug-in word, not really the correct term here but let's work with it, that plagued him as a nine-year-old, concerning being able to deal with sports related stress, especially stress generated by unstated and perhaps, unreal as well, parental expectations. But nonetheless, these expectations were real enough in Walter's mind. Wait a few pages and we will learn a bit more about these mind monsters.

While Walter was quite composed and surprisingly placid when bowling in tournaments and matches at his home court (lanes actually), this, after all, was the finals of the State Junior Bowling Championship and it was a big deal. It was a two-day event and it required a family road trip, a rare event in the Stafford family world, and this road trip would necessitate an overnight stay, which would be a somewhat new experience for the entire Stafford family. Of course, there were exceptions, that being the almost annual one-week family vacation, frequently taken, but not frequently enough to be considered a tradition, and certainly not yearly, and in fact, while vacation traditions might be part of the world of the rich and even those merely of more than modest incomes, incomes quite a bit more than the Stafford's, traditions, such as these were non-existent in the world, in which the Stafford family occupied in the early 1960s. This Stafford family vacation was usually taken in early August and consisted of the family spending six or seven glorious sun-drenched days, typically in a single not special at all motel room, one of those many strip motels you see even today on route 1 in southern Maine, but on several occasions, the family luxuriating in an upgrade to a several bedroom, stand-alone cabin complete with kitchen and screened in porch, a necessity in Maine in late July or early August, mosquitos and sand fly's. These peregrinations were usually to Wells Beach or an adjacent southern Maine beach community. And don't get me wrong, they were glorious and were enjoyed by all!

Walter would be competing in this state championship against seven other youthful bowlers, regional winners representing different geographical areas of the state, and in fact, geographies that were of a much greater population density, far more affluent as well but that unlikely, a major factor in determining bowling excellence, in fact, perhaps, a negative correlation. These regions likely had far more aged twelve to thirteen junior bowlers than New Apley produced, thus, a more competitive environment and likely, Walter would be outclassed and considered a long shot at best to win this event. An interesting tournament fact, perhaps, coincidental, Walter did not, but does now, believe in coincidences, this fact being that all but one of the regional winners in Walter's age-bracket was overweight; this overweight-ness, ranging from moderately fat or considerably overweight (Walter) to grossly obese. No BMI analysis was needed, or existed back in 1963 to demonstrate to all, that the twelve-year boy's division was ripe with obese young men. This fact become immediately evident upon entering the Framingham Bowl, since posted just inside the main entry, this entry being a double set of offset double doors, a virtual airlock, in fact winters were extreme in Framingham and winter was the prime season for bowling, thus, the importance of the simulacrum airlock, but there, posted just beyond this ingression, was a surrealistic display of photographs, not quite Mapplethorpe, but equally disturbing photographs, those pics taken at the roll-offs at each of the regional events. Victory celebrations as well as action shots, were posted in their full 8x10 glossiness, those pics documenting forever, the winning performances of the seven or eight obese twelve years old's, rolling their way onto victory and moving forward onto possible greatness and perhaps, the winning of a state title.

While in the now timeline, it seems that regardless of the athletic endeavor, extreme buff-ness and fitness is a must; mainline sports such as baseball, football etc., so obvious, but this muscle creed has extended itself to sports that were often dominated by slightly chubby beer swilling competitors. Golf, bowling, curling, even, billiards and darts. Colin Montgomery, 'Minnesota Fats', even the 'Babe' arguably the best ball player ever, time-corrected, of course, it was unlikely he could run much farther than the 120 yards required to validate a home run. Bowling Ray Bluth, a big guy but a lot of fat there. In an NPR interview baseball Hall of Famer Wade Boggs, was asked why it seems modern, the interview was likely around 2010, ball players have more injuries today than in the past. His common sense and likely completely accurate answer was, "You can't strain fat!" However, in this past time of 1963, even professional athletes were unlikely to have a personal trainer on their staff or a dedicated seven day a week workout regimen. What the fuck was cross-fit in 1963? A little fat was okay. And in peripheral sports, such as bowling, fitness, and maintaining an appropriate weight or slightly more wasn't even a tertiary consideration. Golf and bowling were not and are not cardiovascular sports. Hand-eye coordination however a must.

The importance, to Walter, as he first entered and insufflated all these new, these visual, these auditory and these olfactory newness(es) of this foreign bowl, of the non-Mapplethorpe photo display, was quite significant and cannot be underplayed. Walter, who was often described at this time as somewhat obese, was one of the most cadaverous and lissome participants competing in the finals of the twelve-year-old division. In fact, it took him far less than, more than a few seconds, to scan the full display and when finished repeat such scan and then focus on the 'thin kid', far from it really, but that 'thin kid', relative, of course, happened to be Walter. Thus, upon accepting this information, the usual baggage or detritus Walter associated with his weight problem, the insecurities, the fretting over, when, or from whom the first or next derisive fat boy call from the peanut gallery disrupting his focus would come, the disapproving looks, the snide commentaries such as "I never knew a fat person could be so athletic," and similar pejoratives were lost. Not an epiphany but this realization was an unexpected but welcomed advantage or maybe just the loss of a disadvantage.

As Walter passed through and beyond his teen years, he lowered his BMI, as well as his bowling average, and often wondered whether a deviation from the norm regarding weight distribution, perhaps, helps in youth bowling, i.e., being fat, would lower the center of gravity of a young bowler, thus, imparting stability the same type of effect one sees in Sumo wrestling. Still only a hypothesis as the younger Walter gave up bowling when he headed off to college, in fact, a year or so before, thus, the importance of the analysis of this possible correlation lost significance.

However, what is of importance, was that an inexplicable and preternatural calm descended upon Walter, descending from the blessed heavens or elsewhere, this calm coming to life and fully enveloping Walter, the moment he viewed that photographic, pornographic, and equally meaningless post of bowling photos.

Today our new 'cyberociety', where even a thought may become a local news story, was not the reality of 1963. In 1963, there would be no posts, no tweets, and no five-minute human-interest stories regarding the seven fat boys vying for a bowling title. Obscurity was a blessing. The seven fat boys, there were actually eight finalists, the one thin kid whom we are completely ignoring and rightly so, did not factor into tournament whatsoever, would go about their two days of bowling; there would be a winner and a runner-up and there would be also-rans.

Regardless of the outcome that Sunday, at the Framingham Bowl, on a fall day in 1963, during the awards ceremony, parents would be proud, the fat boys would be happy, even the also-rans, but come Monday morning as each went back to his respective grammar school, upon their return to that school, the winner, the runner up, and each also ran would again become the object of derision, scorn, contempt, and ridicule. The two-day State Championship would not garner a mention, no special assembly, no mention in home-room period, it was as if it didn't really happen. And this was not or should not have been unexpected; after all, it wasn't as if bowling, even a state championship was a real athletic competition. It wasn't football, basketball, or any of the sports where a white wool sweater with a blue D annealed to the front left surface was the ultimate sign of success.

While it seems our society, our culture, our world, our ethos, or how we define ourselves as the dominant sentient species on this world, has fallen apart, we have become more callous, more vindictive, more cruel, but surprisingly so, at least so in one respect, we have become more compassionate, likely true for at least the 51% or so of non-Trump supporters, this accommodation to decency, being that an acceptance to a general variation from the norm has become more accepted, regardless of whether we are talking about weight, sexual preference, skin color, ethnicity, and a myriad of other attributes, these attributes, which in the past, have created a foundation for hate, separation, and a witch hunting mentality. "Kudos to us!" However, lots more work still to be done!

In Natick, Massachusetts, on that fall night between the first and second day of bowling, for the first and only time in his life, later Ambien episodes not included, young Walter became a somnambulist, arising un-noticed from his bed in the certainly, less than $30 per night Natick Motel the Stafford family, all four, were residing, his sister being there for the finals for the 14-15 year old girls, she, also, being an avid and accomplished bowler, left the room, and as he remembers or has been told so, so many times it seems like a real memory, ambled out onto the second-story balcony of that Motel and commenced practicing his five step approach to the foul line and releasing an imaginary bowling ball, in a Don Carteresque form, very controlled, a slight curve to the ball starting at the third marker, hopefully hitting the pocket and sweeping away all ten pins. This release however, was the mirror image of the Don Carter release, since little Walter was a left-handed bowler, unlike the real Bowling Hall of Famer Don Carter.

At some point, during this middle of the night unscheduled practice session, the elder Walter and Mom noticed Walter's absence, perhaps the Younger made some noise or it was the maternal radar that almost all species, sentient, and those not seem to have. They hurriedly exited the hotel room and upon opening that small, not-quite centrally located door, one can only imagine as to their thoughts as they saw young Walter practicing his approach and release on that imaginary lane, that lane being the not more than five or six feet wide concrete balcony of this cheap motel. They were dumbfounded for sure, stunned into momentary inaction and stood there silently, considering what to do next. After their astonishment subsided a bit, they watched for a bit longer as he, Walter, completed several flawless approaches and releases of his imaginary twelve-pound bowling ball. After watching these several repetitions, and without uttering a word to Walter or each other, Mom and Dad simply and gently ushered Walter back into bed, perhaps, aware he was sleep bowling, but then again, perhaps, simply thinking he was getting in some late-night practice. I only bring up this possibility since the younger Walter didn't follow the norm, in fact, he often created his own syllabus when it came his practice routines.

For a good number of years, Walter spent several hours per day, throwing a golf ball against the concrete front entry steps of the Stafford family home, fielding those balls, which flew back at him much faster than any baseball would in an attempt to become a better fielder, which this practice-routine did accomplish. What these practices did not accomplish, was to instill even a modicum of confidence into Walter, something he was desperately hoping for, in fact, hoping for confidence building beyond just fielding skills, a confidence building for life itself.

Perhaps being a truly good first base-man might help correct or mask at least, deficiencies in other performance areas, which plagued Walter his first two years of Little League baseball and a definite foreshadowing here, the subtitle actually being the obvious foreshadowing, and those deficiencies being a substantial latter part of this narrative.

But no, there was no confidence building, no anxiety reduction, only multiple bruises and contusions the result of speeding golf balls racing back at Walter faster than he and perhaps, any first baseman, regardless of age or skill level, could handle and these balls, without consideration or concern, they were just balls after all, guiltlessly assaulting his body. If, by chance, the thrown golf ball impacted upon those concrete steps at the exact point of meeting between the riser and the tread, the ball would take off in any of many unpredictable directions, Feynman would say all directions, Walter not expecting the bounce and unlikely to be prepared for it and more often than not being unable to field these unexpected missiles and maimed by such bounces. These unpredicted bounces and also just bad tosses missing the steps completely, would, on frequent occasions, result in the breaking of the windows in the Stafford family home entrance, which, in a more grandiose setting, would be called a foyer, but the Stafford's simply called it the front stoop. The windows were replaced frequently, until at some point in time, someone had the fiscally responsible idea to create sort of chicken-wire storm screens to place over the windows when Walter was practicing his fielding. The next morning, upon waking, elder Walter asked his son, "How'd you sleep, son, ready to knock some pins over."

"I guess so," was Walter's response. No clues were provided by this terse commentary, as to his cognition of the previous evening's late-night practice session. Walter's parents did, in fact, know he was sleep-bowling but withheld this information from Walter until after the tournament was over, thinking and rightly so that such news might 'push him over the edge.' While not at a DEFCON 'loss of bladder function' level, Walter was extremely apprehensive, and this resulted in him being unusually quiet; so, simply ignoring until an appropriate time, the events of the previous evening, appeared to be the best course of action.

Other intrusions of psychology and physiology likely led to the sleep bowling episode; most notably, Walter was quite close to the lead after the first day of bowling, a shock and a complete surprise, since, as already expatiated upon, he was clearly not the favorite; several of the other bowlers had rolled games averaging more than thirty pins higher than Walter, these scores posted in the regional event, that adding to his anxiety.

And, to be sure, another not anxiety reducing influence was the fact that Walter had horrible diarrhea from the Friday before the tournament started until post-tournament Sunday afternoon. Nerves, perhaps! Genes, perhaps, no running away from that, although, for most of us, we so determinedly try! Diet induced, most definitely. Walter pretty much had a serious relationship with diarrhea from his first childhood memories until he went off to college, today chronic irritable bowel syndrome is the moniker, then, it was just the 'shits.' Probably the change in his college diet helped. Throughout his freshman college year, Walter embraced the following food groups and this dietary change seemed to help his IBS; those groups being in order of importance, beer, pot, bologna, and pizza. This, in sharp contrast to his home diet, the home being controlled by his mother of Italian ancestry, thus, the typical fare was pasta, lots of cheese, lots of meats, lots of garlic, you get the idea.

Day Two was anti-climactic. Walter bowled as he never bowled before. He averaged thirty points higher than his typical game score. The rest of the fat boys, the only thin one as well, choked. These young superstars typically bowling in the low 200s, barely managed only to score 120 or 130. Young Walter won easily. The longshot came through. Go to the windows and collect on your bets; in this past time, there was no betting in Massachusetts on youth bowling, never has been and likely never will be, but if there, was such a thing, younger Walter would likely have been a 30-1 longshot, so I repeat, go to the windows and cash in your bets, collect your winnings.

On that Sunday afternoon, Butchie graciously accepted his trophy, he did not smile, and was stern faced and we will soon

# Part 3

## Back to Baseball!

The organizational meeting for the New Apley Little League was designed to establish quite a few particulars regarding the league, and after such discussions were concluded, the serious drinking could begin. Coaches were

---

know why at the photo op and awards ceremony; there was quite a substantial gathering of people at the Bowl, well over 100, as all age bracket champions from twelve to eighteen, both, boys and girls were receiving their awards. The ceremony lasted but a few hours, all the Smith's hoping it would finish in time for them to pack up the car and make it home before dark. It did, and they did as well, and as the family drove home, those two plus hours back to New Apley, the assemblage of Smith's were all of a synchronous mindset, they were excited, they were content, they were at one of the few, if not the only apotheosis of life, which the entire family could enjoy. They were, however, not at all, in even the slightest, surprised! The Smith family always owned overly unrealistic expectations regarding younger Walter's performance in a variety, in fact, pretty much any endeavor that the Younger would attempt. PS, Walter's older sister finished a very commendable third in her age group finals, this adding to the spiritual high of the foursome.

assigned to a team, those teams usually sponsored by local businesses and clubs, the elder Walter and Bunsen were assigned to the team sponsored by the Roundabout Society, a social club with chapters throughout North America. Game dates and who played whom was discussed, league rules were reviewed, lots of housekeeping. Of most importance was the draft, this a complicated process which would ultimately determine the official team roster. This small-town Little League draft *was not televised* nor broadcast on any of the then non-existent many sports channels including the ESPN, ESPN2 etc., etc. As society becomes more and more strangled by an ever-increasing array of intrusive forms of media, I do predict that such trivial and daily events, such as local Little League drafts will become at least regionally and perhaps, nationally televised. This will come to pass and why shouldn't it? It's happening now, the other day flipping through channels I tuned into, and quickly tuned off, the first round of play-offs in a Midwest 'corn-hole' league. And I thought *corn-holing* was something pornographic and only happened in rest-stop restrooms! Little did I know it's usually the focal point of many Midwest Independence Day family reunions. All this *will* happen, no buts, butts, perhaps, about it, likely in the not too distant future, and likely on DTV channel, perhaps 49,121.

A baseball draft in towns like New Apley, and New Apley was far from unique, as there were likely many subtle variations of what I am about to describe all across 1960s *America*. Such drafts typically progressed in the following manner. The coaches of each sponsored Little League team, in New Apley typically six to eight teams were able to be fielded from the pool of nine to twelve-year-old boys who had registered, girls were not allowed in these primordial times, were allocated an arbitrary number of points, dollars, credits, cryptocurrency, whatever, just some type of usable *dinero* that they could use to pick or literally purchase their team. The coaches, customarily two for each team, and as each coach likely had a son who would be on the team, the coaches would use these pre-historic bitcoins, the currency of local convention, to buy ten players, to complete their team of twelve from the pool of all the registrants. All the young players, who were registered to participate in the league, were rated and given a 'morning line' dollar value based upon any past performance in the league, performance at the league try-outs, family history, did an older brother participate and how well did he fare, or via some other simply arbitrary, undefinable, ineffable, or what we will collectively call small-town mentality parameters. Perhaps, if the registrant was Italian, the dollar amount increased.[12]

---

[12]This is a true commentary for this time and place, and I am not being glib or disrespectful. New Apley was a town long steeped in Italian and Polish traditions and for many years, most of the local sports stars were of Italian descent. Walter, the Younger, happened to be a little of both, Polish and Italian, and 25% Jewish as well. He only found out about this Jewish connection much later in life, going through some old family papers. Of course, younger Walter lived with his mother's side of the family, several of the members to whom we have been introduced, namely Al and Vera. During these important developmental years, both, Walter and his sister, had minimal contact with his father's side of the family. Elder's mom, Mary, lived only a few blocks away from

New Apley, in the sixties, not unlike many small New England towns had a more than passing interest in baseball, in fact, you might go as far as to call it an obsession. The daily newspaper, The Apley Scribe, had a sports section which accounted for more than half the bulk of the paper with local sports dominating print space. From April

<hr>

Walter's dad's body-shop on Lake Street but contact was rare. Elder's dad, Karl, was of Russian and Austrian descent. Elder Walter was actually named Wladyslaw. Younger Walter had always thought his dad's given name was the Russian cognate, Vladislav, but apparently, they went with the Polish variation. However, it is easy to make the leap to Walter from either the Russian or Polish variant; the Elder's dad, Karl, Stavi…something or other, changed his name to Stafford, a nice sounding Anglo name, upon his arrival, presumably, at Ellis Island and presumably, sometime, in the early twentieth century, however, he was out of the picture, (he died quite young and never met the grandchildren, thus, very little was known about him, a little sad that a life can pass away into forgetfulness so easily,) so it was just Mary, the sole remaining grandparent on the fraternal, I actually mean paternal, but both apply, only in the sense of the 'friendly' definition of fraternal, side of the family. She was a big lady and was of Polish and some other eastern European descent, no *23 and me*™, perhaps far greater specificity, simply passing information on from one generation to the next. As it turned out, her maiden name was Mary Solomon and she was a Polish Jew. This fact was hidden and neither the author, nor Walter can be sure if this was an active or passive hiding of history from the grandchildren. Years later Walter, an older but not the elder Walter, found papers attesting to this Jewish heritage, at the time, he being in his mid-fifties, and sorting through odd and old family papers that his sister had given him.

through early October, each issue detailed the results, including box scores, interviews, and action photographs, of all the local teams from Little League, through high school and beyond. In these transcriptions, you could track the careers of local heroes and trace family histories. Parents of now Little Leaguers would pour through the Scribe, pointing to family names and would exclaim with astonishment or pride, "Look there's Little Anthony Desoto taking after his Dad, you remember, hon, Antony Sr. played with me back in 1950, yea, it was 1950."

Talent seemed to run in families and expectations were always in play. It was expected a Jr. or the rarely encountered III, would create new myths, outdoing the epic tales of his antecessors.

The citizenry of New Apley reached its arithmetic peak with a population of some twenty-five thousand at the turn of the twentieth century; however, that summit has dropped ever since, increasingly more so as of late. Currently, New Apley boasts roughly half as many residents, in spite of a modest recent surge in the economy due to the opening of a not too far away museum of contemporary art. However, in spite of its relatively small size and lack of communal financial resources, thus, an inability to build a fancy stadium, New Apley did, in fact, for a number of years, host a minor league baseball team; several, in fact. Quite an accomplishment for such a small town.

The elder Walter was a locally recognized golfer, having won numerous regional club championships, we already know that. However, beyond just golf, he was a standout athlete in, both, baseball and basketball at St. Frances, one of the three local high schools; two, of which, were parochial schools.[13] While rarely spoken it was obvious to all the Stafford's, the Younger included, that the elder Walter expected or at least hoped younger Walter would follow in his footsteps, carry on the family sports tradition and become a local star in at least one sport, but hopefully more, just like dad. He certainly did not foresee or desire Walter to become gen two at Lakeside Auto Body, higher expectations were certainly in play. However, as the Younger, as early as the tender age of four, started packing on the pounds and embraced divergence from the mean regarding the universal weight-height charts at least at the one or two sigma level, Elder Walter, began to realize that Little League stardom for the Younger was a long-shot at best. The Younger's burgeoning obesity, waistline, and BMI, were not the only problems. Heap onto that, like seconds and thirds of pasta, the Younger was not particularly gifted in hand eye coordination (he was left handed after all, and there is a small group of scientists, not very credible thankfully, who believe left-handedness may

---

[13] Walter the Elder never finished high school, in spite of his athletic prowess. Born in 1914, the Elder would have been a sophomore or junior in high school when the market crash of 1929 occurred and although never spoken of, he likely had to quit school to help support the family, which consisted of his mother Mary and his two sisters. His dad, Walter the Younger's granddad, passed away just about a year before the market crash, thus, Walter the Elder, had to assume the role of family provider, in fact, earning money as a caddy at the previously mentioned Taconic Golf Course, this job helping to provide some cash for himself and his family and more importantly, introducing him to the game.

actually be a form of brain damage), he was quite short (genetics to blame here and perhaps pre-natal smoking or modest alcohol consumption quite common for expectant mothers in the 1950s) and he badly needed corrective lenses, a fact of which no one knew about until four years fast forwarded. And as a topper, as if really anything else was needed to compromise success, he had a bad birthday with respect to Little League. [14]

---

[14] In Little League baseball, you are considered eligible to play as a nine-year-old, if you turn nine years of age no later than July 31 of the year in question. So, for example, if you turned nine years old on August 1, 1959, you were the same age and the baseball equivalent age of a boy who turned nine, 364 days later, actually 365 days, since 1960 was a leap year, having 366 days, July 31, 1960; each boy would be considered a nine-year-old player for the 1960 playing season. One player could essentially be a year older, minus one day, technically, than another boy and still be considered the same age from the league's perspective. While this may not seem to be a big difference, being a year older in any sport, when you were a young and a growing boy, does prove to be a considerable advantage. Walter turned nine on July 11th, therefore, he was a 'young nine-year-old' and therefore, had a *bad* birthday, as he was one of the youngest 'nine-year old's'' in the league. While a bad Little League birthday, July 11th did have its upsides, especially some years later in 1970, when the US government, under Richard Milhous 'Tricky Dick' Nixon, was ordering the drafting of young boys and sending them off to Vietnam to die, to die tragically horrible deaths. Perhaps, and most certainly so, when you are an eighteen-year-old or nineteen or twenty or even a twenty-two-year-old child and sent half-way around the world, and in most cases, against your will, to fight in a war simply created from political motivations, then, perhaps, all

such deaths are horrible, regardless of cause. Dying from friendly fire, dying from hostile fire, dying from booby-traps and landmines, dying from burns the result of napalm being carpet dropped from planes and being used to de-forest large areas of land, so that enemy soldiers could be more easily detected and thus killed, but in doing so, many enemy combatants, civilians, adults, and children, and friendly troops as well, were killed, instantly burning to death in that not quite heavenly fire, and if not immediately dying, likely dying from dehydration, since much of these victim's protective skin had been removed by the burning napalm, or if surviving this, then dying more slowly and painfully via some transmitted disease or parasitic disease infection, etc., etc.

A great number of these useless and needless deaths, most, in fact, were the simple result of randomness; that randomness being based upon a birthday lottery, that lottery deciding who was to live and who was likely to die. On July 1, 1970, the US Selective Service, at 10 a.m., in the morning, held and telecast on ABC its military draft lottery called the 1970 lottery. This was not the first, but the second draft lottery held, as the first lottery was conducted in December of 1969. However, this earlier draft lottery was not telecast, much less ado about something or something like that. This second draft was of paramount importance to Walter, as this draft lottery, concerned all young men, boys, in fact, born in 1951 i.e. Walter. Thus, on that July 1$^{st}$ of 1970, when Walter was eighteen and eligible for the draft, a little plastic two-piece blue ball or capsule, looking somewhat like a large Viagra pill, and that pill-like ball containing the date July 11$^{th}$ within, was pulled out of bingo-like cage A; there were 365 Viagra like blue-balls in this cage, each carrying a single and different day of the year; there would be 365 separate drawings until all dates were pulled. This fateful pull was immediately followed by a second pull from a similar but different bingo-like rotating cage B, this cage also containing blue, plastic Viagra-like balls and these blue almost spherical balls containing the numbers 1 through 365, and this specific extraction of the Viagra-like ball, which would be the draft number assigned to July 11th turned out to be 174. In that year of 1970 because domestic protests were beginning to have an effect on the politicos orchestrating this war, troop deployment to Vietnam and the surrounding countries was de-escalating. An ordered plan for troop removal was in place and because of this, fewer boys were being drafted and sent off to die. In fact, in Walter's year of draft eligibility, only boys with numbers up to 125 would be called. So, during this summer day in 1970, sometime late morning, watching the draft with his friends, Howie and Robert, Walter was most definitely happy; happy doesn't begin to convey the shade or intensity of emotion here. Howie and Robert were happy as well as they had even higher numbers, to have that bad Little League birthday when July 11th was accorded the draft number of 174. No Vietnam for Walter or even having to worry about pre-induction physicals.

*Wait, stop, reconsider, edit needed here!* Before we go on, we need more information; this ineffable, instant euphoric happiness I am attempting and failing to describe or convey, didn't actually happen on that July 1st late morning, perhaps, early afternoon. When Walter's birthday was pulled out of that bingo-like or lottery-like cage as number 174, at the moment when that number was pulled, it was not possible to predict if the draft would cover birthdays with this number or higher. In fact, in the previous year boys were drafted with numbers up to 195. So, no there was no instant happiness, no euphoria, however, no trauma either; 174 was in the nether region. Walter would have to wait about four months until it became clear that numbers from this lottery no greater than 125 would be called for pre-induction physicals.

From the preserved recollections of younger Walter and from every source this author has been able to access, first-hand, second-hand, and beyond, it appears with certainty that the Elder Walter was a very laid-back dude, mellow, relaxed, insouciant, pliable, placid, and was exceedingly calm, even before he began his nightly ritual of downing, pretty much coincidentally, with his entrance through the front door of the family home on Whitway Street, his one or two and perhaps more, as younger Walter may have edited this memory, his beloved Gordon's gin, usually in the form of a gin Rickey or gin and tonic, never a gin martini; thus, never shaken nor stirred. Laid back was never a term used in these past times; it is an anachronism for that time at least, but not now, actually, that term seemed to have its fifteen minutes of fame in the 1970s and 1980s, nevertheless, that (laid back), the elder Walter was. It was also an uncontestable fact, unverifiable as well, that the elder often went with the flow or followed the path of least resistance, a team player was he. A malleable, amenable, and a very agreeable man, could have done well in California, where *manana* is just a day away. Walter, the elder, was a solid citizen, a true adult, the kind of adult that seemed to have sprung up post WWII, and these real men who became the norm, were the quintessential dads throughout the 1950s. These average, yet emblematic, men were movie heroes, they were TV dads, they were role models, they demanded respect, in spite of the fact they were not exceptional and had countless flaws; they smoked,

---

Hallelujah, a somewhat delayed, but certainly momentous euphoria!

they drank, and they may have harbored less than laudatory expectations for their spouses. However, they were American heroes, post-war heroes building a generation. They were venerated; perhaps unduly so, but thus they were. Unlike today, where a corporate title or an eight-figure net worth is necessary to command any attention and perhaps, respect whatsoever, if it even exists today, these everyday dads were to be looked up to and emulated. Walter's dad was the embodiment of this every day, nameless American hero. Persistence, commitment, and no recognition. Hollywood has useless award ceremonies every two weeks for meaningless entertainment activities, but where is the recognition of consistent parenting which helped generate those eight-figured successes and far more, less financially, but of truly greater import solid citizens. None forthcoming, rant ended!

Walter, the elder, was the perfect dad, flawless, at least when he was with his son and as painted and recorded by the younger Walter's brushes and canvas. Adventures included in their father-son time together, over the many years, defining the entirety of younger Walter's childhood, were the numerous rounds of golf, several years of organized and just pick-up baseball, family outings, picnics, quite a few trips to the drive-in to see the latest Hollywood release, most of these gatherings local but still of importance, and of course, their almost, but not quite annual trips to Maine. We can add to that, many pilgrimages the entire family would make to Green Mountain Park, just a few miles from New Apley across the state line in Vermont, the nightly home to quite a few New Apley residents, as well as the time spent bowling and other at Mt. Fetlock

Bowl. These times were father-son, Walter-Walter bonding times, not quite unique, but as different as they were the same, coming of age experiences, hopefully, resulting in the boy becoming the man.

What stands out, remarkably so to the younger Walter, perhaps in Technicolor™ is during each and all of these Walter-Walter bonding times, the younger Walter had very few, if any occasions, none in fact, to observe from his so even tempered dad any outrage or anger or even the slightest hint, a molecule, an atom, or even a quark of a verbalized expression of displeasure or anger, perhaps, an occasional damn or 'Oh Shit', but certainly never, never, never, ever, ever, never until this first and only time an "Oh fuck!" [15]

_______________________

[15] In fact, younger Walter does recall hearing his father, who was an outstanding local golfer, winning several club championships, including one at the very elite Taconic Country Club in 1949 and to this day, if you now ask the older younger Walter, he will proudly show you the gold key chain decorated with six raised golf clubs that was awarded to the elder Walter for his victory that year and on another occasion, shooting a 66-67 to win a 36-hole Club Championship in Pittsfield Massachusetts, saying *fuck* actually just once.

This notable moment came to be while playing a round of golf, dad and son, and two other men of no significance and certainly not possible to determine who they were at this time, and most certainly deceased, as they were more or less Walter's father's age, DOB circa 1914. This unforgettable round of golf was played on a former cow pasture, converted into a simple nine-hole course, just across the Massachusetts state line in Stanfry, Vermont, a likely three or four dollars a round course back then, and about fifteen minutes from the Stafford home. Dad and son played there quite often, sometimes, with younger Walter's sister. And if you are wondering or asking, and the answer is yes, you could still smell the cows, who were simply relocated a short distance onto land adjacent to the course. And another yes, you could also smell the decomposed by-products from the tons of manure gifted by those cows or their antecedents to the course over many years before the course opened, and even before the idea of turning this pastoral setting into a modest, nine-hole golf course sparked into existence.

For years, these fecund rolling pastures were blessed with the most lush and greenest of grass, that grass indigenous to southern New England and thriving without supervision or significant intervention, and this grass, simply being what grew in this part of New England, unlikely to have a name, a pedigree or a provenance.

But a golf course, even a nine-hole, four-dollar a round course in southern Vermont in the early 1960s must have a turf designed specifically for golf. Lush green, orphan grass simply will not do. This verdant valley was torn asunder and highly inbred and golf specific bent grass, likely Colonial Bent Agrostis capilaris, replaced, much to the chagrin of the adjacent cows, the unknown grass, which had provided nourishment to these gentle creatures for many a few years.

This evolved species of flora required much more than the water provided by the local microclimate of southern Vermont and more nutrients than found in the decomposed manure bestowed free of charge by the former residents of this formerly lovely green paradise. Accordingly, this Stanfry course, even with newly installed Colonial Bent grass, did not sport the plush wonderful green expanses we expect to see today at the $300-500 per round courses, those named and admired destinations, repetitively appearing on the bucket list of many a few golfers. However, those lush green expanses we expect to see, but did not see at the local 1960s Stanfry golf course, do not exist because of some divine knowledge gleaned from the Turf Management Program at Rutgers University or some other more prestigious learning institution; *no*, they exist only because of the invention and actual use of copious amounts of nitrogen-based fertilizers, which can and have been used for acts of terrorism and then again tons of pesticides, created synthetically, most perhaps in New Jersey and spewing off many kilograms of toxic waste into the local rivers as a by-product and causing, unprovable, of course, who knows how many cancers. Add to that the constant manicuring of the greens and fairways with assorted very inefficient and noisy gas powered turf grooming devices, my opinion only, but if alive today, Dante would have added a tenth circle of Hell, that belonging to the inventor of, as well as the libertine users of these gas powered nightmares, usually operating on Monday, the universal off-day for most private courses, or in the early hours of the morning. Adding those together all those activities, that's how the wonderful green expanses, oh, I almost forgot, let's also add the thousands of gallons of water, which is, if you believe the scientific experts with no hidden agendas and not the politicians, likely becoming an endangered resource, magically appear. Alas but not at the Stanfry Club. The grass was thin and sketchy, winter rules were always in play. Again, remember this was the 1960s and the peripheral Berkshire Mountain area was then, not what it is today, in terms of being an attraction to the wealthy and elite. The owners of this hapless course simply could not afford to resort to these measures to recreate the lovely green expanses that existed effortlessly, long before the revitalization of this valley occurred, and became an attraction for those who could not afford more than four dollars for a round of golf. Simply a matter of ROI, return on investment! However, the manure rich fairways of Stanfry Country Club did attract flies.

The *Oh fuck* came after Walter, the Elder, made an errant drive, something he literally never did! And Walter does mean, in fact, never. In the hundreds of rounds of golf younger and elder Walter played, perhaps over a five or six-year span encompassing younger Walters's passage from twelve to eighteen, the Younger cannot recall a single occasion whereby Elder's drive did not go straight down the middle of the fairway. Of course, there must have been a few bad drives, but those occasions were so isolated that the memory of Walter the Younger, surely has expunged them. Walter the Elder, was not a terribly long hitter, sort of a Cory Pavin type, thus, the ability to hit the fairway consistently is more readily explainable and believable. Walter has no recollection of which hole the *Oh fuck* hole was, golf holes are numbered one through eighteen, nine in this case as Stanfry was only a nine-hole course; in order to record an eighteen-hole round, the standard round in golf, you had to play the course twice, from different tees, i.e. different starting positions, so the course played slightly differently the second-nine. He also has no exact recollection regarding the errant drive as to why it prompted the Elder to utter this forbidden execration; did the drive go out of bounds incurring essentially a two-stroke penalty, actually stroke and distance, which is tantamount to a two-stroke penalty, did it enter a lateral hazard, here a real one stroke penalty, or did it simply not live up to the elder Walter's expectations. This unimportant information long forgotten.

Why then an *Oh Fuck?* It was a meaningless round of golf, younger Walter was never judgmental with respect to the elder Walter's game or anything else about his Dad or family for that manner; nothing but true unconditional love. He realized his father was getting older and after working 50-60 hard hours per week re-shaping, sanding, compounding, and painting pieces of automobiles deformed by collisions with animate or inanimate objects back into good enough but certainly not perfection, and then after work, relaxing with two or three shots of Gordon's gin, not straight, a gin Rickey, or on the rocks with lime. After twenty years of this and smoking two to three packs of cigarettes a day, Marlboro's and then, when money, which was always scarce, became even tighter rolling his own cigarettes, each morning at the small rectangular, linoleum kitchen table, after awakening the entire household with his morning hack, the hack that long term smokers typically have, and it was simply random, whether the first hack of the day was the elder Walter's or his wife's or younger Walter's Uncle Al, as they all were since their teen years chronically addicted smokers and each one greeted the day with that sputum infused hack that was all too familiar to younger Walter and thus, younger Walter, with his habit of studying and analyzing others from a distance, and being somewhat insightful about and having a harbinging understanding of biology and the human body and in spite of the overwhelming built in denial systems we develop to void any chinks in familial armor, the Younger realized that Elder's game was not what it used to be, because his dad was physically much older than he was chronologically and was deteriorating pretty rapidly, therefore, there was no judgment, perhaps just a little sadness when the elder Walter hit a bad shot. So, I ask again why then the *Oh fuck?*

What we do know and can be completely certain of is the look of shock on the younger Walter's naïve and infantine face upon hearing the first utterance of that henceforth forbidden dysphemism, *fuck,* forbidden, at least, in younger Walter's mind. You might think big deal an *Oh Fuck,* a thousand times a day, every day in this world of 20xy; we are exposed to this invective in the movies, all forms of media; in fact, preschoolers even, have become desensitized to an occasional or perhaps an overload of *fuck.* However, to put in proper context and especially for the younger readers, a digression is needed here as to the evolution over time of the word *fuck* itself, with respect to general usage, then and today, and especially to place into context its general usage in rural, somewhat, isolated 1960s Western Massachusetts. Walter himself never verbalized *fuck,* not at least so others could hear him, until he was in the seventh grade, now considered Jr. High School, but at that time part of the K-8 system, in a school named Fetlock Elementary School, by the way, still in existence in New Apley Massachusetts but now only K through 7. *Fuck* was a taboo, an unspoken word, in New Apley in the 1960s; this was true for its intended use in any of its forms, verb, noun, adjective, interjection, adverb; nor was it used when an entirely unexpected event occurred, whether life threatening, painful, annoying, or just plain startling. Hit your thumb with a hammer, *oh shit,* maybe, never *oh fuck,* trip and fall on your face, *Jesus Christ, Mother of God* perhaps, not *oh fuck,* bird shits on your head, Damn, not an *oh fuck.* Someone pisses you off, your response would not be go *fuck* yourself or *fuck-off,* douchebag, it might have been *piss off, douchebag.* You complete your tenth sixty-yard sprint, bend over, rest your forearms on your thighs in complete exhaustion, not being able to lift your head, never mind run another sprint, sure, today, a barely audible or a primarily screamed *oh fuck* is expected. In fact, today Walter rates his workout intensity based upon the number of *oh fuck* moments that arise in a thirty-minute cross-fit set. Back then, it was *shit* or 'damn that hurts.' As a modifier, I am really tired, not I'm *fucking* tired! I've got a *fuckload* of work to do, no, maybe a *shitload.* Something goes wrong and you have no recourse, you might be screwed, but you certainly are not *fucked.* Certainly, no *motherfuckers, fucknuts,* or *fuckwads.*

Of course, the returning war vets, any war, pick one, had their share of *fuck* exposure as the verb, noun, and adjective. SNAFU an acronym arguably originating during World War II and arguably created by a Mr. Anonymous in the Marine Corps, point in case. The acronym stands for 'Situation Normal: All Fucked

Up.' However, often fouled up replaced the offending fucked. In fact, the army produced training films describing the misadventures, presumably so the young draftees could avoid such mishaps of a Private Snafu. As these videos are now impossible to find, the author cannot determine if the fucked or fouled was used in these productions.

To say it was never used is clearly an over statement, however, it was not used in the world of the Younger and as far as the Younger recalls, the elder Walter's world either. Of course, those students at Dreary Regional High School, several years older than Walter, were likely using the fuck word, perhaps not the *oh fuck*, but the seniors, the high school elite, mostly Italians and jocks, were using the fuck word for what it was meant to be used; a verb form, a synonym for getting laid, they were fucking their brains out, and fucking like bunnies; this fuck, the verb form, was a world, word as well, unfamiliar to Walter then, and for quite a few more years, in fact, a few more years than he dearly wished.

It will never be known why elder Walter uttered the *Oh Fuck*, thus, creating a defining moment in time, at least in younger Walter's mind. Perhaps it was intentional, perhaps it was meaningless, perhaps, unknown to younger Walter, his Dad said fuck all the time. Fuck you, fuck this fucking sandpaper, give me a fucking gin, fuck Al, fucking government, my fucking son is driving me fucking batty, I hope he finally swings at that fucking ball, a hope he grows a fucking pair, many possibilities. For sure younger Walter has overthought this point in time to ad nauseam and sadly no answer was or will be forthcoming. However, the utterance created a moment, an epiphany, an afflatus, scribed into the conscious and unconscious mind of the younger Walter. After the oh *fuck* on the surface, all was pretty much the same, no uncomfortable or awkward silences, to all, it might have seemed the event never happened, there seemed to be no real ramifications. Walter still played golf with his Dad, but less so,

Thus, the backstory has been set. Elder Walter was certainly not an alpha-male, but he was hard working, he kept his nose to the grindstone, he drank a little too much and unquestionably, he adored and doted upon his only son, and this son being somewhat of an enigma. Hence, from a real perspective, this pretty decent dad applied little, if any, significant or noticeable pressure to younger Walter concerning his Little League performance. Especially true since this year would be the younger Walter's first year in any form of organized baseball or sports whatsoever. In these past times, back in New Apley, in the 1960s, there did not exist, as does now, imitations of youth baseball, such as coach or dad underhand pitch or T-ball, these less than

---

twice a week, morphed to weekly, then, perhaps, twice a month. They still tossed the ball back and forth, usually pre-dinner, but again as with golf, less and less frequently as the days passed. While conversation was always sparse and mostly about school, it continued without change. Were these changes the result of the *oh fuck* or simply timing, the separation of younger Walter from the roost? Unknown for sure, but perhaps, his Dad, on some level, recognized the importance of the *oh fuck* the shattering of an ideal, the less than perfect man, now appearing less than perfect to his far from perfect son. Perhaps, the elder Walter knew, the Younger as well, there would be more errant drives, an inevitable realization we will all eventually come to, whether it be a golf shot or some other event of importance; the inescapable result of the simple passage of time combined with the needless and necessary exposure to the toxins and the intoxicants of life. A mystery of life, meaningless, but not, at least, for a few, one, at least, unimportant and small and not to be resolved here, only reflected upon.

organized 'games' starting when these infantile less than ball-playing, ballplayers are, perhaps, five or six years of age. In these puerile undertakings of today, crying is allowed, and in fact, sometimes, encouraged. But no, no changing history, thus, this first season of Little League would be the Younger's first year participation in any form of organized team sports. The Elder being a very practical man, sometimes to a fault, realized putting pressure on his only son would be of no value, would only make things worse, and he knew that. He accepted that a subpar performance was in the cards and he was determined to ignore it for all he was worth.

While Mom ruled the house and this rule was totalitarian in almost all aspects of family life, when it came to sports, she sat in the back seat and the Elder did the proverbial driving. Of course, in spite of all my above declarations, the family did hope, mom might have even prayed to whatever Catholic deity is responsible for sports, for nothing less than stardom for the Younger, even as a nine-year-old Little Leaguer; it's pretty much a universal parenting trait; hopes and desires define predictions. Perhaps, more than just a parental attribute, we often expect what we wish, not what we should truly, expect to happen as rational, but only part of the time, beings.

Of course, these unrealistically high expectations for Walter, in all and every aspect of life, regardless of the absurdity of such expectations, were kept hidden from younger Walter, at least, his parents completely incorrectly or delusionally thought so. Visible and stated expectations were generally reserved for all things academic, which, as the days passed, the younger exhibited an ever-growing talent therein. And praise was typically given only well *after* an accomplishment or achievement, the parents were quite aware of the Younger's insecurities. Nine-year-old Walter was a good student, far above average, but he had not reached the lofty heights of academic prowess that he would rise to in high school and throughout college and post college academia. They, the parents, gently pushed, provided opportunities, encouraged, never impugned failure, and were tolerant of his sometimes-questionable wishes. For example, what nine-year-old wants a copy of Don Quixote as a birthday present. Certainly, an outlier, but, *no*, the book was purchased, it was not read until three or four years later, but today, this then $1.95 priced and prized Penguin Classic, translated by J. M. Cohen has been re-read numerous times and sits on one of the many shelves, none housing birds or other results of taxidermy, in Walter's current library.

Walter trying to be objective, can now look back in time, those almost fifty or so years, and admit that his parents were always supportive, never negative, and in fact, their support of the Younger didn't border on, but often went far beyond delusional. Was this bad or detrimental parenting? Perhaps, perhaps not, only time will or has told!

Thus, the facts are not really the facts, and perhaps, what is, is not what is, but is what's not; therefore, denying the reality of what actually happened or what was real and true, as viewed by the Stafford's from any angle of their observation, and often in spite of very apparent contrarian facts, the Younger was absolutely, unconditionally, categorically, undeniably, and irrefutably perfect. Their world allowed for no other possibility, nothing whatsoever.

And this deification was well recognized by the Younger and of the course the Younger could not but react to it.

So let's forget the non-facts, on some deeper level, Walter, the budding scientist, was also a realist; is any real scientist not one after all? Thus, Walter did experience extreme parental pressure concerning his performance. Pressures, perhaps, not expressed but definitely sensed and perceived by his overly large introspective mind. And as days passed, these internally generated pressures were greatly magnified and growing exponentially each time young Walter chose to reflect upon them, yet, in spite of this Walter chose to spend more and more time reflecting upon these unstated expectations becoming somewhat obsessed. In fact, he turned more and more inward and would relive most inconsequential and meaningless daily interactions, viewing each from afar, searching for alternative meanings to straightforward commentary, and role playing, he playing himself as well as his parents, and continuing conversations in his mind to numerous conclusions, most fantastical, many disparaging to himself, however, the end result was most of these inner-directed dramas simply fortified his belief that

1) His success in everything was of paramount importance to his beloved parents, and

2) He was simply not worthy to live up to these internally created Dickensian expectations.

There were many reasons, some real and others not-real, but there were enough real reasons to make it utterly impossible for nine-year old Walter not to live in a world wherein he existed in the depths, wallowing about in the mud, and primordial sludge of self-pity and fear. He did have his defenses, defenses as they were, however, his shabbily constructed and easily folded house of card's escutcheon was barely one-dimensional and only existed fleetingly, and mostly in his mind, and only then, *sans* human companionship and potential confrontation.

Daily engagements resulted in the slings and arrows of reality being introduced into Walter's heretofore sheltered existence. These penetrating vectors of blindingly clear, accurate, but unfathomable information, were being delivered now on a daily basis and originating for many directions. No longer was it simply the reassurances of the Stafford's shaping Walter's quotidian existence.

As time passes, the child-parent bond weakens and dissociates, as is to be expected. Our so-called lesser counterparts seem to do it better. After all, just push the baby bird out of the nest. Nature takes care of the rest. The unconditional and sometimes irrational support system, providing the basis of the perfection and infallibility of the younger Walter ebbed. The no longer to be avoided external views and opinions were coming into play. Walter was on his own and he could no longer hide in the rooms of his elaborately created mind mansion.

Teachers, classmates, teammates, friends, only a few, more likely bumped into acquaintances, were rating Walter constantly on physical appearance, clothing, hobbies, who your friends or 'crew' were, not a term even in existence back then, but certainly a concept, who your parents were or what they did, in what sport you excelled, in other words, the baggage you carried from the previous years of existence in this small town. Let's not even get into having the 'wrong kind of body' whether real or a body image perception.

Today being rated is an integral aspect of life, not so much so in the near past. In, now, time, have your car serviced and a multitude of emails spring forth. Are you happy with the overall experience? When did an oil change necessitate filling out a form which demanded the use of no. 2 pencil and consisted of more questions than a late 1960s SAT test? Sorry, that's my only experiential reference. And when did an oil change become an experience? Make a reservation to dine somewhere through one of the many available dining apps, and until you provide detailed feedback, good or bad, it doesn't matter, it's just bytes of information, you are under electronic assault, endlessly attacked by an electromagnetic inquisition. However, not to be hypocritical, I was quite happy to be solicited for feedback when we unfortunately chose a new, local tapas restaurant called Picador, one mid-week summer evening, several years past. My short and terse electronic response, when my comments were requested via the ubiquitous infobahn was simply "Pick another door!" Whether my comments were influential or not, undeterminable, however, I am happy to report Picador closed its doors shortly after they opened. These examples are but a few on the list of requests for feedback, that list growing daily, and it seems spam filters and do-not-call lists do not work. In today's world, more time might be spent giving feedback than getting serviced.

But even in this past world, a real world, not a fictional world, the younger Walter's world, ratings from outsiders were recognized and relevant and impacted the Younger more and more, especially true as the unpredictable dance of life pulled the Younger farther and farther away from the all protective Stafford family womb. However, unlike today, most of these ratings were direct or somewhat direct at least, backstabbing certainly was not direct, and was in play in this past-time as it always has been, "Eh, Brutus?", but it didn't involve emails, tweets, or texts, and clearly was not delivered, nor received through the bodiless electronic web.

Ratings, in these past times, were pretty clear and often quite frank. Good was good, bad was bad, fat was fat, being an outsider was not being an insider, deviation from the norm with respect to any visible physical characteristics, whether ears, eyes, nose, teeth, or body odor provided reasons for derision, scorn, mockery, and disdain, perhaps, physical abuse as well, and most definitely social isolation.

Walter, while not really a big fan of sailing, was nonetheless quite familiar with that three-thousand-mile-long African monster, known as 'da Nile,' and while the turrets and walls of his castle were well-guarded, the drawbridge regrettably had not been raised and the main gate to the castle was left open. The enemy had to simply walk straight into the mind of the nine-year-old Walter. These enemy soldiers, took an overland route, avoiding denial and introduced themselves directly and impacting the young fat nine-year-old like chestnuts falling into slightly softened butter on a warm summer day.

These cleverly disguised soldiers bore the names of fatty, fatso, fat boy, chubs, porky, pig boy, porky, 'porko', and many more. Of course, being fat automatically tagged your family as being fair game for any and all possible forms of denigration. Bored, intolerant, xenophobic herd mentality driven nine-year old's can be quite creative with respect to verbal abuse. However, let's be clear, much of the creatively did originate from the equally, if not more so, racist, world hardened, misanthropic, malevolent, and morose parents.

So needless to say, but actually, absolutely required to be stated, younger nine-year-old Walter, in spite of parental affirmations and contrived self-delusion, when you came down to it, carried with him an inferiority complex, so immense that if carried by Atlas himself and he happened to shrug, that shrug would have resulted in a crushing and annihilating blow, reducing this Titan to mere godly detritus scattered about the floor.

The younger Walter does not recall or perhaps, chooses not to recall, the precise enlightening moment he realized he was fat and thus the dawn of the FBI (Fat-Based Insecurity). Those above-mentioned soldiers of obesity certainly hastened his enlightenment, but when exactly that happened, can not to be established with certainty and really what does preciseness matter anyway. It happened! Thank you, Monsieur Heisenberg!

A fat child is always a fat child and therefore, must become a fat adult, and as the author has posited before what is real is often not real, body image is pretty much fixed at a young age. Older Younger Walter reacting to the FBI, at some point in his mid-twenties, morphed into a dedicated exerholic, which, surprisingly, is a word and not rejected by the omnipotent spell check, and continued to be such and became even more fanatical, as he traveled into and through what we will loosely call old age; in other words, real time now. But despite a very low BMI, a low-fat percentage, likely six percent or so, and a relatively high muscle content, this very fit and quite thin older Younger Walter still considers himself a fat boy. Yes, crazy indeed, but a classic example of body-dysmorphic disorder.

Behavioral research has shown that adrenaline acts like cement and can fix or permanentize our memories. Accordingly, whatever happens when you are in danger, frightened, agitated, or under high stress, results in memories that are highly preserved and more likely to be recalled and reflected upon compared with other memories created under serene, less-stressful conditions. Therefore, it makes perfect sense that these stressful, troublesome, painful, and disturbing childhood memories will likely dominate and occupy a substantially greater portion of one's childhood recollections. No wonder we are so collectively fucked up today! While younger Walter had many pleasant childhood experiences, we, now, can understand why he dwells on the not too few unpleasant experiences.

So, what's the big deal, so you're fat, it's not like that being fat isn't the norm today. Statistics suggest that today one out of every five nine-year old's is obese. And let's remember, obese is an extreme category. Younger Walter frequently changed teams during his developmental years, switching from the chubbies, to the quite fat, to the not quite morbidly obese. So, in the now, it is likely one out of every three nine-year-old is parity on the fat scale with the then nine-year-old Walter. However, today is not yesterday but today. And what we can be absolutely sure of is that obesity is far more common and is less of a social concern today than it is was in rural, 1960s western Massachusetts. In those past times, in that faraway place, if you were obese, you stood out. Both adults and children called you fat. As you walked away and to your face. You didn't have to split your overly tight, hand-me-down pants in front of the class, while giving a presentation or not be able to secure the bottoms of your Little League uniform when they were handed out to you at the first meeting of the Roundabout team, and later that evening, your mother had to add a button extension onto those bottoms, to be ridiculed, but events like that certainly helped. Farting during a class presentation helped also. While the author has not done the research, it seems likely that thin people fart as often as fat people. Farting has nothing to do with weight, body mass, or calorie intake but is directly related to gut microbiology. But let's all be honest, it is far more funny, especially for adolescents, for a fat bugger to fart than a thin one.

When buying clothes, which the Stafford family did infrequently, but when such an event did occur, they were quietly ushered to the husky section of Richards' Clothing Store. The husky section was less substantial, a purposeful pun here and substantial referring to the available selection of clothes, not their size, than you might think. These shopping events were rare, as more commonly, the late summer, pre-school new clothes shopping experience consisted of sorting through the hand-me-downs from somewhat chubby but not fat nor obese cousin Bobby. Something to his credit, Walter felt no shame or embarrassment when wearing these familial gifts, in fact, he remembers fondly and with excitement receiving these donations and spending hours in front of the only mirror in the house, an inexpensive, perhaps, two by five-foot silvered piece of glass, likely distorting all images, not a bad thing for Walter, and going through each precious acquisition and sorting them into two piles, 'public' or 'home only.'

It wasn't only obesity that annihilated the younger Walter's self-image, however, it certainly was, no doubt the major actor; but this play was not a soliloquy, there was a supporting cast, and within that supportive group, the most important character, adding onto and enhancing the strength of the FBI, was Walter's less than desirable dental aesthetics.

Younger Walter desperately needed the skills of an exceptional orthodontist, probably quite apparent to all, including the Younger, as early as at the age of nine or ten. Fact simple, his mouth was far too small for his teeth. No blame to be placed there, other than an inopportune meeting of genes.

Walter to this day remembers, but not fondly, and he still has the photo to memorialize, an Easter photo taken perhaps in 1960, the rookie Little League year, this photo of the main family of four, the family appropriately decked out in their traditional Catholic Easter garb, posed, but not so poised, on the balcony of their grandmother's, mother's side of the family of course, apartment, on the third level of what today or perhaps, even yesterday, would or might be called a tenement apartment.

It was a typical family holiday photo; repeated far too many times, by far too many families, most likely, far more of these shots taken in the far away 1950s and 1960s than today, but then again, perhaps not, and I have no data or facts to support either hypothesis, likely the only true statement we can make, is today, almost all of such images are digital, of course. These oft repeated pictures were of somewhat identical, idyllic families, celebrating important rites of the Catholic religion.

The Stafford family were Roman Catholics with a decidedly Roman emphasis and were not overly religious, but nonetheless, Sunday mass was a requirement, unless it interfered with seasonal bowling. Participation in the Church's not so pagan holidays and the various prescribed rites of passage, such as Communion and Confirmation were also absolutely required. The most striking and memorable aspect of this unique photo is that, in this picture, Walter was actually smiling, sporting a teeth evidencing grin, bearing all, the instant that Kodak moment was made, something he rarely, and definitely purposefully, *would never do*. Thus, that Easter photo was, and is still a record permanent, or for as long as it exists, and it still exists in the now, not in a shoe box, but in a photo album of assorted Stafford Family Memories, of his misaligned, crowded, distorted, anfractuous, misshapen, gnarled, tortile, crammed, catawampus upper-teeth.

In the developing mouth of the younger Walter, the canine teeth, the cuspids, arguably the most important teeth in fixing the upper triplex arch structure, came late to the party, obviously busy doing something else, arriving far later than the other teeth, clearly showing their superior role in the toothy hierarchy, but in doing so, they simply had no room to make their grand entrance. However, desiring a prominent location, they, nevertheless, decided to simply move forward, crowd their way into and onto ongoing conversations, and sit on top of the incisors, Mr. and Mrs., the lateral on each side, pushing forward and outward and titling, perhaps, as much as thirty degrees from the normal plane of the remainder of the fangs and thus, causing quite a bit of discomfort for the incisors, the Mr. and Mrs. Not a pretty site to be held for sure. But younger Walter was not exceptional in this physical deformity, this was a not an uncommon occurrence. No, he wasn't one in a million, possibly, one in several hundred at most. This happened all the time and even in rural Massachusetts and fixes for such physical deformities did exist.

The older, younger Walter has on many occasions oft stated, no, perhaps pedantically affirmed, to his wife, children, and business associates, or pretty much anyone who will listen to his occasional rants, that the merely competent will often be quite successful, as the majority of society that one encounters, and in general, doesn't quite make it to that level, quite subpar in fact. "Be thankful for the lazy and the stupid," I have often heard Walter profess, "They make it easier for the rest of us to succeed." Regrettably, when it came time to choose a dentist for the Younger, and very few options were available in New Apley at the time, the family choice was clearly one of the many in that above-mentioned grouping, those that would make it easy for the merely competent to succeed.

The brain surgeon the Stafford family chose to become the guardian to and of the younger's teeth and by virtue of this, such appointee having a substantial role in the development of the Younger's psyche, was not a brain surgeon at all, he actually was a board-certified dentist, but as we shall learn, not a very competent one.

As results may dictate our impressions of things past and completely blind us to the long forgotten truths, it is possible this qualified DDM, who ended up prescribing a disastrous dentalcare regimen for the Younger, may have actually recommended that braces were in order for younger Walter and might have under different circumstances, or perhaps, going there again, sorry, in another of the infinite multiverses, been quite competent. However, we only have an n=1 to adjudge by.

He might have aggressively opined this corrective course of action, unlikely, but let's cut this long, dead hack some slack. However, braces and a visit to an orthodontist, who would have likely proscribed a quite reasonable, long-term, and unreasonably expensive plan for the Younger's teeth would not happen. Any reasonable or other plan, would in *lieu* of extracting teeth, have extracted a quite substantial sum of money from the Stafford family, money, which the family did not have nor could have obtained.

Options unrealistic and fantastical might have been available, allowing the family to amass such monies. Perhaps, the elder Walter could have sold a kidney, not really an option back then, I'm not sure kidney transplants were done with any frequency in 1960; someone please Google that. The Elder was an ardent follower of the ponies, if his fortunes were favorable, he might have hit it big, perhaps, cashing in on a 100-1 shot at the local Green Mountain Race track or betting with one of the few bookies with whom he spent less than considerable time. But, alas, such a payday was as likely to happen, as selling the aforementioned kidney. And, of course, neither of those did happen; ergo, directions were given to the aforementioned cranial surgeon to move forward as he saw fit, without the intervention of any specialized treatments from the highly recommended and quite pricey orthodontist.

Braces were immediately ruled out, not just for financial reasons, mainly, yes, but also because Walter's mother, who was in-charge of pretty much all housekeeping matters, including dental care, insisted, and Walter now knows this insistence was a defensive and coping strategy to avoid the fact that the Stafford family was unable to afford orthodontic care, and the defense and diffusive strategy Walter's mother proffered was that braces weaken your basic tooth structure and will weaken the root, pronounced as 'rut' by the entire Stafford family and also by an older younger Walter, until he consciously chose not to, structure and lead to tooth loss; therefore, no braces for Walter.

This rejection of the solid idea of braces, resulted in a course of action we will simply call the good enough approach. This approach, concocted by the aforementioned brain surgeon, in *lieu* of proper and somewhat expensive dental care, was simply to remove a few extraneous or redundant teeth here or there, haphazardly, not thought out very well either, but good enough.

It's quite astonishing that this brain surgeon felt that symmetry wasn't very important in determining the future of younger Walter's smile. A canine here, a bicuspid there, perfection and symmetry highly over-rated!

This good enough approach was as follows. Rather than perhaps removing the first bicuspid on each the upper-left and right quadrants of Walter's mouth, the cranial specialist chose to remove a canine on the right side; that being one of the canines so rudely arriving late to the mouth party; and a second removal being an upper lateral incisor on the other side, that being the left side, the Mrs. Incisor referred to also above.

On Walter's lower teeth, only a single canine was removed, this time the left side, fifty-fifty chance of that happening. Only this single tooth was removed, no other pearls were taken from the lower level.

Since only a single tooth was extracted, this brain surgeon clearly felt that crowding on this ground floor, was not as prominent, not true, or perhaps, less visible, also, not true, or simply not of importance; after all, Walter was the son of a man who painted cars and removed dents from those cars, prior to painting, certainly less than great expectations were in play, so a good enough approach to dentalcare seemed completely appropriate. Symmetry highly overrated, this also not true, as now only a single canine remained on the ground floor! So good enough!

These extractions took place over a very short period of time, no more than two or three weeks. Walter emerged from these extractions with just a jumble of teeth, no symmetry, and the pearly soldiers in no way standing in attendance, facing all which ways, and without external guidance, just not knowing what to do next.

This good-enough approach, with minimal follow up over the following few years, simply resulted in Walter having really bad teeth from an aesthetics perspective and function as well. Still overcrowding in some places, gaps in others, and the mandible soldiers facing to all points of the compass. A photo might be appropriate here, but alas, we know about that, just one ever existed, and now, it seems, that even that aforementioned Easter photo, which, until just now, was a record permanent of the atrocity described above, while apparently becoming more yellow each day and the image fading with time like a bad memory, that photo, we so want to see, has disappeared, just as do so many of our most and least favorite memories. So, you are just going to have to take my word as to enormity of the cluster-fuck that was younger Walter's mouth during and beyond the start of his Little League adventures.

# Part 4

## The TIT 1969 and the Blind Date

Moving on, but not back to Little League, and leaving behind this slightly morbid dental diversion, it must be obvious now, even to the most obtuse or the disinterested, younger Walter's somewhat misshapen, gnarled, unbalanced, and simply hideous smile; noted, reference to DFW here, generated a shit-storm of emotional mines, as in minefields, and each one of these mines was likely to be triggered by the most common of everyday passings.

Some of these detonations were trivial, others not quite so. The less than trivial events, of which, there were more than a few, will be ignored, since most are inconsequential in the 'big picture.' However, before our return to baseball, we will elaborate upon a more than trivial gnarled dentifrice event, a somewhat important integral, perhaps, an Ignatius J. Reilly moment, this digression adding a few more strokes of paint to the Walter canvas, but in doing so, delaying our return to baseball.

In this somewhat lengthy diversion from the great American pastime, Walter was a college freshman, living at the 'Tute,' the somewhat archaic terminology for the mythical Troy Institute of Technology, also referred to, and most regrettably so, as the TIT[16].

Walter does not recall the exact date, and it not being important, perhaps, October, but it definitely was sometime in the early days of his first college semester, that being the fall of 1969, and to his pleasant surprise, the rarified and implausible opportunity for a blind date with a supposedly lovely, young freshman coed from Sagamore College materialized.[17]

---

[16]It's hard to fathom what higher power chose the name Troy Institute of Technology as the moniker for a technical school that would morph into a top-tier generation spanning institute of higher learning. When founded in the early nineteenth century, acronyms must have existed. Did tit mean tit back then? Were people just so serious not to realize that whatever multisyllabic title the school actually bore would, eventually, be reduced to an acronym fully associated with the fairer gender's most striking attribute? Red and grey T-shirts emblazoned with TIT. Football season, 'the TIT's take the field.' During the time, younger Walter attended the Tute, the TIT actually had a quite impressive soccer team. 'The TITs score another goal.' Lose a few games and how can you not proclaim for all to hear 'The TITs seem to be sagging a bit this year.' However, would the Polytechnic Institute of Troy be any better? Yes, Troy was the pits but why announce it to the world. "I go to PIT in Troy, which, by the way, is the pits." Not much better. But as expounded elsewhere, you can't unwrite what had been written. Walter was a TIT and he loved it! And he loved Troy as well!

[17] The enrolling freshman class at TIT in 1969 had SAT scores in math well over 700 and verbal, as it was called back then, slightly over 600. The entering class was made up of about 1,000 students, 950 being male and as a TIT freshman, you were more likely to

Walter, as a TIT freshman student, had a car. He was not supposed to have one, but he did have a car. The vehicle prohibition for freshmen is true and a given at most Universities and Colleges. Clearly, a car is a distraction to these less than full, competent, complete, rational (whatever) adults and this car will simply distract these eighteen and nineteen-year-old embryos from accomplishing the two tasks they have matriculated for at their college or university of choice. Number one being getting excellent grades in whatever academic field they have chosen to specialize in and number two being, perhaps, it's number one actually, to get laid! In fact, a car would be of a definite advantage for this latter objective.

Walter, the Elder, was in the automotive business, so it seemed quite reasonable that college-aged Walter should avail himself of any advantage, possible to make up for his personal shortages, perceived and real, in so many other important aspects of life. And being a freshman with a car, especially at the TIT with a male to female ratio of 19:1, was a definite advantage.[18]

---

be a class valedictorian than a sports star or even having participated in a high school varsity sport. That being said, the opportunity for a date, any date, including a blind one, was very welcomed, even considering TIT was approximately 30 miles south of Sagamore College, which was located in the lovely horse racing town, a town Walter was quite familiar with, Saratoga, NY.

[18] Irony is a bitch. As it turned out, college-aged Walter ended up dating, senior-year, second semester and marrying one of those 50 TIT entering class of 1969 coeds, Jeannie. One Saturday night in January of their senior year, Jeannie was a blind date of his next-door hall mate, George; there they met, started dating shortly

The car that Walter brought to the TIT was a 1966 Peugeot 404, and it was awesome! Walter's father had bought it at a used car auction in Windsor-Locks, Connecticut, sometime before Walter, the Younger, headed off to college, the cost about $400. This was a considerable amount of money for the Stafford's back then. Likely, two or more weeks' worth of his dad's take-home pay. The car needed a lot of work. It was a joint summer project for both Waters, but mostly the Elder, as the Younger was unquestionably a distraction, his skills were limited. It, the Peugeot, had a three-speed stick on the steering column, it had no ABS, no power steering, no power brakes, or a nav system, no Bluetooth connectivity, no six pack DVD holder, no six or eight-way power seats, no Shiatsu massage function, no power windows, *and* no cup holders. It did have ash disposal devices, I believe they were called ashtrays, at several prominent locations and an AM radio with four buttons, with which you could use to program your AM station of choice. It had leather-like, beige vinyl bucket seats, two in front and a bench seat in the rear. The dash, door trim, and all accents were a faded burgundy red. It had about thirty thousand miles on the odometer when purchased, however, since in those past times, all you needed was a drill and the appropriate bit to turn back an odometer, something Walter the Younger and the Elder did countless times, who really knew what the mileage was. It was point and click just like a camera! It had no seatbelts,

---

thereafter, began living together more shortly thereafter, and eventually, getting married, less than nine months later. And today, the clock is still turning; together for forty-six plus years.

they were not required in the US until 1968, and then, on new cars only, and retrofitting was not necessary, but it did have a sunroof, mechanical with a crank. It actually was a snow-roof, since whenever there was a winter storm in Troy, NY, of which, there were many, spring and fall snowstorms as well, Walter and his roommate at the time, Vinny, a quite jovial far more mature than Walter and a very Italian Vinny from Long Island with parents of questionable provenance, would hop in the car, sometimes stoned, sometimes not, more likely than not stoned, rapidly accelerate, tires skidding and spinning in place, no such thing as all-weather tires or a slip-differential in 1969, get up to a considerable and under the conditions a clearly unsafe speed, and without a thought as to the ramifications, crank open that snow roof and luxuriate in the sheer pleasure and stupidity of being blinded by sometimes up to eighteen inches of snow, tens of millions of diamond like crystals, each different, as we all know, falling through that two by two and a half-foot dimensional opening, while they, Walter and Vinny, travelling sightlessly and thoughtlessly at, perhaps up to sixty miles per hour on the snow-covered roads of Troy. Walter driving blind, unknowingly, unwittingly, without responsibility, he and Vinny just enjoying that moment in time, pure pleasure, thoughtless pleasure, remarkable pleasure. Thankfully, nary an untoward consequence occurred.

On other snowy and boring weekends, the Peugeot and Walter *sans* Vinny, just the two, Walter and the French Lion, passed an indeterminable amount of time, doing and repeating figure eights, on the snow and ice-covered empty parking lots of Troy High School, just across Fifteenth

Street from the dorms. These completely drug free escapades were a must, well, drug free, most or some of the time at least; they were also undefinably pleasurable and thoughtless and were indispensable adventures and escapes at the time. Now, looking back through time, these exploits were stupid, foolhardy, mindless, feckless, reckless, imprudent, hair-brained and temerarious, but viscerally unmatchable and fortunately non-consequential pleasures that would be hard to match today in our much less safe world, a world with far more severe consequences.

TIT was not an easy school back in 1969. More than one third of the freshman class dropped out before year's end.[19] These snowy adventures were mindless releases, defiance of the system, a breaking out from the norm, and were absolutely essential, at least, for Walter, allowing him to survive in this new highly competitive and very different college world, a world 'unfathomly' different and far more unpredictable from the one younger Walter had spent the past eighteen years.

It, the Peugeot, was two-tone green, painted by, both, Walter the Younger and the Elder at Lakeside Auto-body. The two shades of green would be difficult to describe in terms other than puke and pus, but on this car, they worked. Walter painstakingly applied a beige pinstripe, perhaps, six inches below the lower boundary of the vehicle's front and

---

[19] Walter vividly remembers a short presentation at freshman orientation, by who unknown, and it doesn't really matter, but the point of consequence was the following words from this unknown speaker, "Ladies and gentlemen, look to your left, look to your right, one of you three will not graduate from this fine institute."

rear windows; it was a four-door sedan. This, pinstriping, was 'all the rage' back then. Walter owned the vehicle, actually, used is accurate, as the title was in the name of Lakeside Auto-body, for a bit more than two years and put close to twenty thousand miles on it. Other than gasoline, which was pretty inexpensive back then, and a few oil changes, the car was a quite inexpensive ride; little, if any, maintenance was needed.[20]

The last time Walter exited that magical vehicle, after those twenty thousand or so carefree miles, most times driving not so cautiously, doing reckless figure eights, driving far in excess of recommended speeds, ignoring weather conditions, and let's not forget trips started and finished, without the slightest idea as to who was piloting the French Lion, 'snow roof' precipitated avalanches and other snowy adventures, with and without Vinny, the exit was not through a door, rather the front windshield served as the final point of egress. Thankfully, that thin but suitably strong piece of glass, shattered as it should have, thus allowing Walter to continue his adventures at the TIT and beyond. This final Lion trek started in Troy and ended, the last end, in fact, in Albany, New York, in 1971, two years in the future from this Sagamore blind date event and many years in the future, almost a lifetime, from the Little League Walter, the adventures thereof, which this narrative is

---

[20] This might not be true, what I am meaning to say was little if any maintenance was actually performed on the vehicle, whether it was needed or not, in all likelihood, the car needed unperformed maintenance(s), including at least a new set of tires and certainly a break job, long before its partnership with Walter ended.

mostly or arguably concerned with. Walter was, during that last journey, escorting in the aforementioned pus-puke conveyance, and indeed a rare occasion, a young lady, a nurse, another blind date, actually, there were many, her name regrettably unknown now, once known and long forgotten; she residing somewhere in Albany, about ten miles from the 'Tute.' Walter was driving her in the Peugeot, back to her abode, from a John McLaughlin concert held at the TIT Skate-house. She, the John McLaughlin nurse, was a spin-off of another blind date this date arranged by roommate Vinny. Vinny was dating a roommate of Walter's blind date. *And yes, it is confusing.* For the record, a spin-off blind date, at least in this case, and there may be countless alternative definitions, is the roommate, perhaps, a friend or acquaintance works as well, of a person you actually have the blind date with and for the spin-off date to come to life, you reject a follow up date, seriously, Walter rejecting a follow up date, unbelievable but in this case, yes, true, with the original date, and go ahead and date her roommate. Confusing, for sure and further explanation follows. There were three nurses and they were roommates, all residing in a small two-bedroom apartment, brick, kind of a row house, half flight walkup, somewhere in Albany. Vinny, procured the original date with, let's just call her nurse number one and Walter ended up dating the two other nurses, first nurse, number two, she being the blind date, orchestrated by Vinny and this was his first date within this circle of nurses. Upon their return to the nurse's apartment from that first date, the four of them, Vinny, Walter, and the two nurses, number one and two, the foursome decided to engage in whatever activities young nurses and TIT males engage in. During this awkward, fumbling about, Walter happened to meet nurse number three, and in spite of having quite a good time with nurse number two, he and number three 'hit it off.' Clearly fate had some master plan in store for Walter and nurse number three.

And as fate dictates and fate does, in fact, dictate all, the original blind date, she was blond, as were all three nurses, but quite easy to tell apart, whether sober (unlikely) or drunk (almost surely, and it didn't matter who was drunk the nurses or Walter or Vinny for the proper identifications to be made), nevertheless, she, nurse number two, while being the loser in the Walter 'no second date lottery' ended up being the overall winner. Brings to mind something, can't quite place the meaning or reference Pyrrhic victories?

Why Walter rejected a follow up date with this quite attractive, willing, and mindless nurse number two, and opted for the spin-off date with number three eludes Walter even to this day, clearly as espoused throughout this narrative 'fate.'

As things turned out spin-off date, nurse number three, also exited through the windshield of the Peugeot 404, as it was T-boned, hit on the passenger's side by a non-descript Ford pick-up truck, at a somewhat prominent Albany intersection, exact location forever lost, but less than a few blocks from the apartment of these three soon to be two nurses. She, nurse number three, was not wearing a seatbelt, as there were none in that 1966 of French origin vehicle. Upon impact with the Ford, control of the Peugeot was lost, a new directional vector at a slightly reduced speed was taken; it, the Peugeot, losing momentum, kinetic energy, velocity etc., a concession perhaps for the nerds here, and the vehicle continuing on this new and unanticipated vector, only slowly reducing speed as by this time Walter was nowhere near any vehicular controls and in all likelihood, concussed. Eventually, the out of control Peugeot continued on a straight line until it made its acquaintance with a very solid, rebar reinforced cinder block wall, that wall being the lower half of a not unusual but quite standard, fare Laundromat. Upon meeting that wall, the Peugeot decelerated from a speed of perhaps fifteen or twenty miles per hour to zero miles per hour, zero whatever per whatever works just as well, in but a distance of perhaps three or four feet, and in, perhaps, a tenth of a second or less. You do the math, actually not an option for most, but the math is scary. What's scary is this completely unpredicted and unforeseen sudden stop, resulted in possibly, a greater than 10g deceleration, a traumatic and disruptive one for sure, but not necessarily a fatal one. Fortuitously, in spite of this close to lethal deceleration, one of the two youthful and blissfully unaware projectiles, both being launched through the front windscreen, did survive this 10g deceleration, including passage, through thankfully, shatter-proof glass and not too softly landing on the hood of the fatally injured French Lion. No smiles or hallucinated winks from the Lion that night! Walter has no recollection whatsoever of that evening's events after his launch through the front windshield. He does recall some events pre-launch, tightly holding onto the steering wheel, actually hands at the two and ten position, and upon impact with the cinderblock wall, rotating counterclockwise, and being launched headfirst over the steering wheel and the back, left side of his head providing the force to pass through that French-produced front windshield.

His next moment of sentience, was waking up in the Troy Hospital ER, neck secured in an alien like brace, he having fractured his C5 vertebrae, and nearby, an officer of the law, possibly NY State Police, patiently waiting, waiting to ask Walter a few questions, questions then and now, that he had (has) little or no recollection of, the officer, hoping Walter could provide some clarification of the events of that earlier evening.

Sometime later, Vinny, Vinny without a smile, on that early morning, whatever day, escorted Walter back to the dorms and together, over the next few months, the two of them attempted and succeeded in consuming well over several thousand 714s, Walter for, perhaps, a bonafide medical purpose, and Vinny simply because he was Vinny!

A sobering result of the unavoidable events of that fateful evening was that of the three actors in his short tragedy, the Lion, the Nurse, and Walter, only one survived and that being a somewhat surprising feat in itself![21]

---

[21] Fate clearly wanted Walter to avoid this deadly event and attempted to intervene, but alas, as with so many time travelers in so many fictional stories it has been shown, that it's simply not possible to change the history that has been written or more apropos, perhaps, to re-write the future that may have already been written. More than one traveler in time has failed to prevent L.H.O. from shooting J.F.K. on that N. day in 1963 or intervene in other such events of historic proportions. And again, in this case, with the Lion, Walter, and the Nurse, taking the stage, fate failed to intervene, to change the course of future history, and write, perhaps, a gentler tale. In the Walter story, as he and the

windshield nurse began their ill-fated journey back to the Albany residence of the three young nurses, the two of them being, perhaps, somewhat intoxicated, but then again, possibly not, they entered the happy Peugeot and proceeded in their Chariot, heading down the hill from the Wallace Hall Dorms, Walter's residence of choice in this his junior year at the TIT, heading towards Fifteenth Street, and the hill being quite an angled slope. Walter applied the brakes near the bottom of the hill, and in his possibly somewhat diminished capacity, but then again, perhaps not, he proclaimed, "The brakes seem to be off, perhaps we should return to my abode and complete this journey in the a.m." The young nurse, having heard and seen far more than Walter could ever then and even now have elocuted, saw through this rookie ploy and insisted upon a now return. Walter, accepting the rejection of a stay-over, returned to his room, rousted the soundly sleeping of provenance questionable roommate, Vinny, and after quite serenely listening to a few minutes' worth of expletives, simply asked Vinny for the keys to his 1970 Camaro, engine cc displacement unknown but it was *hot* and of considerable displacement! Favor granted, wasn't even a question of being rejected in these past times, today, questionable. However, with keys in hand, younger Walter and the windshield nurse quietly made their way back to the car, the Camaro, not the Peugeot, it, the Peugeot, inanimately biding its time, not at all feeling rejected, it simply sat nearby, after all, it was simply a car, a composite of metal and plastic. The two not quite lovers entered the vehicle, fastened their seatbelts, yes, this was a 1970 GM, one of its finest they built, at a time when GM was a brand to be reckoned with. It was a fully safety provisioned vehicle with functional seatbelts. Walter started the car, threw it into gear, and rapidly accelerated down the hill, and with a helping, or perhaps, a heaping, of *déjà vu*, they re-began their journey towards fifteen street. Regrettably a short venture, it would be as within but a few seconds a flashing red light exploded upon the dash, that light indicating 'Danger Will Robinson', no, not quite, but almost as bad, the message being 'Caution low fuel immediately refuel.'

Time and circumstances dictate every response, whether the response ends up being optimal, logical, or just plain stupid. On this particular Saturday p.m. in Troy NY, it was no longer Saturday, but was now a.m. Sunday, the likelihood of finding an open gas station was naught. Besides, Walter wasn't particularly interested in throwing, perhaps, five or so dollars' worth of petrol into the fuel tank of the obviously considerably more, well-off Vinny; gasoline cost about thirty cents per gallon back then, so arguably Walter could have gotten away with spending less than a dollar if he could find an open fuel stop. Nevertheless, there would be no refueling, and back to option one. Thus, another scene change and back to the Peugeot we go.

Things progressed quite nicely, the journey that is, egress from the Wallace Hall parking lot, down the hill, onto Fifteenth Street, and across the Hudson River, proceeding towards Albany, all without incidence. So far so good. There were no brake issues, the Lion was behaving himself. Albany was within sight and within seconds, the nurses' apartment was also in sight. All was good until sometime after two a.m., when both the Peugeot and another vehicle, this other vehicle being a Ford truck of considerably more heft, entered the same intersection on this early Sunday morning in Albany, NY, and both these vehicles attempted that always unsuccessful physics experiment, that experiment, being put into a question 'what happens when two objects try to occupy the same space at the same time?' Where's Heisenberg when you need him?

It was a straight through intersection, four vectors proceeding towards a single point, Walter approaching from the south and the Ford truck from the east. There was a light, of course, it was a main intersection. As Walter approached such, the green light

But, now, back to Sagamore and 1969.

This blind date, the Sagamore blind date, and we are now back in 1969, Walter's freshman year was memorable and worthy of further details, so let's expand upon it, not as a footnote, which was the author's original intent, but as a more than minor digression from the main narrative, and I promise we will get back to baseball and I believe you will find this tale worthy of additional narration. Even Billy Pilgrim might get nauseous from all this time unsticking! [22]

This blind date, not the fateful Peugeot ending date of 1971 but this earlier 1969 date, narrative now time, was arranged by a dorm mate, Nathan Hall, and this is the name of the dorm itself, not the name of the young man who lived across the hall on the second floor room number 20x, where x equals an odd number from one to nine, trying to be a bit cryptic; the dorm mate's name was Barry, he was Jewish, he was tall, he was un-healthfully thin, not fit thin, he had bad acne, he had dark hair, the hair appeared dirty and greasy, even after showering he was a bit slimy, clearly, he was producing excess sebum during these adolescent days

---

turned yellow, he applied the brakes of the smiling Lion and they, the brakes, without a doubt, or perhaps, a definite maybe, they failed, failed completely, not the slightest reduction in velocity noted. The Lion proceeded though the intersection and was struck on the right side and let's keep the metaphor fresh, it was struck by a rhinoceros of a vehicle. The results, of which, are more fully described within the main body of this narrative.

[22] Billy Pilgrim is a fictional anti-hero of Slaughterhouse Five. Wartime trauma (WWII) causes him to become unstuck in time and he travels throughout time, somewhat, randomly, thought driven, similar to the flow of this narrative.

and could have used something to tame this oil production but sorry, Retin A™ was not available in 1969, he slouched, never really stood tall, slinked a bit when he walked, you know what I mean, a lot more hip motion than you would expect from a guy, especially in 1969, today, you might say he was gay, simply upon observing his body language, only an observation, not a pejorative, but he was in active pursuit of a Sagamore College coed, so go figure; how he actually managed to get a date was a mystery to Walter, although Walter was clearly not an expert with respect to dating and male-female dynamics. Walter believed the Sagamore date was arranged by a friend of a friend of a friend back home. Nevertheless, Barry did have a pending date and needed a plus one and consequently, 'Walter the car,' was obviously the top choice for wingman. Sagamore College was in Saratoga, New York and as noted previously, some thirty plus miles distant, well beyond any non-existent mass transit in upstate New York during the time we are talking about. Barry did not have a car, he came from the Bronx, Co-Op City to be exact, completely self-sustained, or it was designed to be, by intent, so you never had to leave the complex; today that sounds like a winning idea. It was quite dangerous in the South Bronx back then; Co-op City was the predominantly New York Jewish take on Ayn Rand's Galt's Gulch, it's unlikely that any of Barry's family members or past generations owned a motor vehicle of any sort. I cannot be sure of future generations…if there were any!

The date was made, it was a Saturday night and Barry and Walter would drive in the magical Peugeot to Saratoga, leaving the TIT about five p.m., driving about five miles west and then taking the Northway (Interstate 87) and driving the twenty five or so miles to Saratoga and arriving at about six, no Waze or apps to help but distance travelled and time expectations were pretty predictable back in the late 1960s, fewer cars on the road, better (less distracted) drivers. Upon their arrival, it was previously arranged by Barry that they would meet the girls at their freshman dorm and then proceed to the Café Lena, a local bar, coffee shop, and small concert venue for local and even well-known folk artists, Don McLean did appear there, not that night and an event Walter regrettably missed and he, Don, performed, and by all reports, it was transcendental, his generational hit 'American Pie.' Café Lena was on a side street, Phila Street, off the main street, right in the middle of the downtown, one of the many streets, upon which, you could make a sharp right turn onto, if you were heading north on this main drag Broadway, and proceed down quite a steep slope, these side streets housing a diversity of businesses not quite up to main drag quality.

Today, Saratoga is somewhat of an upscale, upstate New York village. It has spa's, at least one spa, perhaps more, Saratoga Spring Water is well known for its purported healing properties and was likely served at the pre-eminent local spa the Gideon Putnam Hotel, which originated in 1802 as the Grand Union Boarding House founded by the above-mentioned GP, fine restaurants, and mediocre hotels, one of them being the location of a hilarious episode from a book by Johnathan Ames, who, in this author's opinion, developed one of TV's all-time best sitcoms. By the way, Café Lena is still doing what it did some fifty years ago and is now referred to as the legendary Café Lena. No disagreement here!

All these small businesses, far more than you might expect for a town the size of Saratoga are supported by the rich, the famous, and the not so famous or wealthy race track aficionados, who simply feel that August in Saratoga, NY, is the equine equivalent of December in Bethlehem. To many of these fans, "You have to be there."

Walter was there, for many years in fact, pre-and post-narrative, he started watching the ponies, as little Butchie with his parents at Green Mountain Park, a track as similar to Saratoga as a jar of pickles is to a Klein Bottle. And indeed, it, Saratoga, *was* the equine equivalent of Bethlehem, featuring at one time or the other, all of racing's Triple Crown winners, some winning, others losing, all of them since 1948. Five Triple Crown winners starting in 1948 with Citation and currently holding with American Pharoah 2015[23], and *yes*, this is the correct spelling, well,

---

[23] Time is flying faster than the ink is drying on the pages of this somewhat lengthening short story, so we must amend. Justify has just won the Triple Crown, current reference June 2018. While I don't expect to see other amendments as I sincerely hope that my musings will not rival the realm of William Gass, who, arguably, took thirty years to finish the Tunnel, by the way, it took me less than a half hour to finish reading that book, but I ended on p. 23 I believe. Just last week, Justify won the last leg, the Belmont Stakes becoming the second Triple Crown winner in three years. As of this date, he has not appeared at Saratoga, but it is possible he will do so in the coming months necessitating a further foot-note. It seems Triple Crown winners come in groups, the future TBD.

for the horse at least, perhaps the owner was lysdexic (dyslexic), an ailment the younger Walter was most definitely and still is affected with.

In 1969, these steeply, sloping side streets were filled with small businesses, housed in old pre-1950s, mostly brick two story structures, usually with a somewhat narrow and slightly dangerous set of concrete steps edged by a code required wrought iron railing leading to an underground reality housing and doing who knows what, but the main and upper levels of these dilapidated and decaying structures specialized in selling used clothing, candles, vinyl discs, which also happened to play music if you so owned the appropriate decoding device, fishing and hunting gear, more used clothing, moo moo's and tie-died attire, pretty much the uniform for, perhaps, half a generation and the requisite attire if you were a 'dead-head', 'head-shops' abounded, those stores supporting the then and now still illegal, somewhere definitely, probably Republican states only, it is changing rapidly, and rampant and largely ignored use of marijuana, these shops selling rolling paper, roach clips, black lights, posters, mostly Jimi Hendrix and Pink Floyd, which would come alive under illumination from these black lights and even more so if you were under the influence of tetrahydrocannabinol. Also available for purchase were an assortment of low-tech pipes, ranging from corn cob, brings to mind Super Ray, to simple blown glass pipes, fashioned from a single piece of glass, metal pipes fashioned in a similar manner, to first generation bongs, unfashionable Hookahs, they were not popular in the late sixties and early seventies, today, however(???), and an assortment of lab inspired water pipes. These lab creations were the smoking devices of choice, as you might expect for most of the technology and science-oriented students who happened to be attending the TIT during this time and had a passing interest in the recreational pleasures of Miss Mary Jane, access also important, rubber tubing, flasks, funnels easy to smuggle out of O-chem lab down in Wesley Hall. But let's not forget one-hitters, also known as *Kiersu* (Japan), *chillums* (Nepal) or *sebsi* (Morocco); Walter believes, although widely available for centuries in other cultures, such devices were not at all common in Troy, NY in the late 1960s, and perhaps did not exist in those days, although he can't be certain.

Barry and Walter were to meet the coeds at their dorm, a dorm within the Sagamore College community, occupying the northern portion of the village, east of the main street. The name of the dorm and other many other trivial details have long since evaporated from Walter's memory, only room for the important stuff! Parking was at a premium at Sagamore and this was true at most campuses, especially at the freshman dorm area, since it was pretty much a universal given that vehicles for freshman at any school were verboten!

There were no convenient parking spaces available, without literally having to walk a distance equal to the distance the group would have had to travel to reach Café Lena, so Walter waited in the Peugeot in front of the dorm, engine idling readying for his (their) escapade, maybe, escape; Barry would make first contact, he seemed totally self-assured which astounded Walter, as he knew Barry was not exactly a ladies man[24]. Barry retrieved the two young ladies seemingly completely at ease, Walter was impressed. Barry was pretty tall and the girls were but a few inches shorter, Walter was fretting over the possibility he might be the shortest of the foursome. The threesome made their way to the Peugeot, and introductions were made, Walter-Louise, Louise-Walter, Walter-some other girl, some other girl-Walter. There seemed to be some nervousness evident from each of the group of four. Walter did not leave the driver's seat, he didn't jump out of the vehicle and greet this arriving group, *no*, he was probably too frightened to move, he was not trying to be cool, didn't know how to be such, nonetheless, his behavior was one that one might have been mistakenly interpreted as being cool. Cool and terror-struck are often opposite ends of the spectrum, complete antilogies, that can often be confused from afar. Casual and feigned aloofness versus genuine terror. His, Walter's, attention was focused on the road in front, as if he were driving at great speeds on the autobahn, even though, at this point in time, his vehicle was still in park. Hands at ten and two o'clock, head barely turning to acknowledge the arrival of the three plus. Just a nod of the head as a recognition of the status change. When all passengers were secured in the magical Peugeot, Louise in the front seat next to Walter and

---

[24] A few years later, Walter found out that Barry was in fact quite the lady's man. He was a great guitarist, his acne was history and he had joined a band, Hymie Rabinowitz and the C City Rastas, and made a few bucks as well as punched quite a few tickets (euphemism here) doing gigs at Bat Mitzvahs, not ever having to leave Co-Op City. Fuck, yes!

Barry and the other girl in the back, without hesitation or caution, Walter floored the accelerator launching the four cylinder 150 HP Peugeot quickly up to speeds of perhaps fifty miles per hour, but for just a few seconds, when, of course, almost instantly, they had reached the less than a half mile away Café Lena and upon arrival, they immediately found a spot to deposit the car, spots, of which, there were many.

Who knows, I surely don't, what these two freshman Sagamore coeds were expecting or hoping for when they agreed to and showed up for a double-blind date with two TIT freshmen, likely described as somewhat nerdy engineering, pre-engineering, or science students. More likely, there were no descriptions, that's how things happened before the invention of social media. In today's world, everything is known about almost everyone, there is no blindness in a blind date of today. Is the term even in use today?

What was the motivation for these far more sophisticated and aware 'chadults' (child/adults my own word here) to even agree to go on such a date with Barry and Walter? Boredom, a social experiment, a few free drinks, as if they needed such, the male half of the date generally paid back then, this last thought, unlikely a factor. Such silliness! Granted Sagamore had the same but antipodal demographic issues as TIT. Some five hundred to six hundred students, all young ladies, no men enrolled at that time; these students likely feeling as if cloistered in the 1969 version of a nineteenth century monastery. On campus, the only male contact being the student-teacher interactions with male professors/instructors, arguably, perhaps more than half of these being straight. And fortunately, for some of these young girls, at least some, and I'm sure more than just a few, teaching tended at this time to be very hands on and such handiness was not so frowned upon as it is today. No, it was generally ignored and perhaps considered one of the perks not found in the employee guidebook, if such a thing existed. So, perhaps, some diversions. It's also likely the high school boyfriends of many of these young ladies had found a long-distance relationship hard to keep up, this likely being the only thing they found hard to keep up and thus, they had disappeared from the scene. Apart from this sexual apartheid, Sagamore was physically isolated as well, the nearest Ivy being, perhaps, a five-hour drive. Williams College, a 'Little Ivy' was only an hour away from Sagamore, but honestly, Mt. Holyoke, Bennington, and Smith College were just as close to Williams, and frankly, the girls at those three schools likely had SAT scores far more compatible with those found at Williams; seriously, you're considering this, SAT scores, you may ask? Well, peripherally, yes, but also, for the record, the girls at these schools, were just as isolated, just as desirous of male companionship, and these other schools could be considered the feminine social equivalent of the mostly male Little Ivies, so, yes. Certainly more so than Sagamore and its student body(ies). So, retracing and retracting, let's revise here, the TIT wasn't that bad an option for these girls. Far better than 'dudes' from Albany State, Onion College; actually, Union, a local joke, or Plattsburg.

However, one would have to stretch their imagination quite far to think that these two young ladies did not, for an instant, ask, perhaps look up to whatever deity or higher power they believed in and screamed thusly, "Who have we wronged?" proclaiming this, the instant upon meeting the not too greasy Barry and the inanimate, and ADA representative Walter[25]. Whether it was Walter and Barry, Matt and Tom, Stan and Sol, or Duane and Darwin, it was unlikely that any two TIT male freshman and any two Sagamore co-eds would be a likely match.

TIT was, sadly, the TIT; it was a technology-based institute and ranked high on the nerd radar. SAT scores well over 700 in math, at a time when SAT scores were meaningful, lots of valedictorians, lots of science medal, and Westinghouse Science Award winners. Social skills and graces were lacking in most of the matriculated TIT freshman (over 90% male). TIT was likely a safety school for a few students; those who desired to go to Cal Tech or MIT and didn't quite cut it or have the right connections, but this was not true for Walter. He was a science and technology enthusiast and whether intentional or by lucky randomness, the guidance staff at Drumly Regional High School had a few previous successes placing the school's top students at the TIT, and most of these students, receiving substantial funds in a variety of forms, thus, for Walter, the TIT was a 'no-brainer.'

It likely took Walter more time to park the Peugeot, precisely centering the vehicle between the white lines, defining the outer dimensions and boundaries of the spot

---

[25] ADA refers to the American Dental Association, not the American's with Disabilities Act which did not exist in this past-time, as it was created in 1990.

itself, than it took to drive into town, he was overly cautious, at least when sober, of his precious possession. Parking completed and the group of four, regrettably, sober, not stoned, not on the sublime guidance of Quaaludes, Rorer's 714, methaqualone, no alcohol buzz, not having imbibed any godly elixir, they, thusly, proceeded forth completely and blindingly cognizant, aware, and unimpaired. A harsh reality indeed and one that had to envelop a major cultural and socio-economic gap between these four souls, as these souls, were, in some sense, bound together, unless one or more of them had the courage to make it otherwise so for the next several hours.

Scene change—Interior Café Lena

A table was found, drinks were ordered, and magically appeared without delay, folk music played in the background, recorded music, non-descript, not Muzak, or a playlist, likely an LP or cassette, and not from the group that would soon take the stage, mellow getting to know each other music, Joan Baez, Joni Mitchell, and the like. It, the current world of these four students, was noisy, it smelled like beer, it was smoky, it, the smoky smell, was, regrettably tobacco, not pot, it (this) was a college town, but it was 1969 after all, and all this was to be expected.

The blind date was blonde and not blind, excellent vision and stunning blue eyes, and whose name Walter no longer remembers (really), but for a place keeper, we will assign to that character the name Louise, Walter, knowing for a fact, that Louise was not the name of the young lady we are discussing; it's fascinating that while we might not be able to positively assign the correct name to something or someone, we almost always know when that name is not correct. Repeat this iteration thousands of times and you will always get the correct answer. But let's pass on that, this is likely a case where a presumed or assigned name works best!

Walter was not omniscient nor an optician, but knew, without doubt, that this newly met young lady had excellent vision. This knowledge alighted onto his consciousness, upon commencement of the first substantive verbal interaction within the group, the first utterance of any words in fact, from any within that group, the group of four mismatched souls, in the dimly lit, quite noisy and smoky Café Lena, in Saratoga, NY in 1969. This utterance that was of such import and was proffered by this very tall (tall, in 1969, for a young lady was perhaps five feet, eight inches tall, Walter's height, maybe a bit more, her height, not his, but certainly not tall in current chronology) and attractive, not classically so, but in a way, for which, the proper adjective eludes me now, but I will re-state for emphasis *very* attractive; pale, thin, angular, a sharp skeletal definition, David Bowie-like, temporarily out of sequence perhaps, maybe asexual, not the date herself but her look, and certainly an upper middle class young lady (insert your own description here, if you choose to) and Walter does recall to this very day that this quite attractive young lady was from Newton (or maybe Wellesley) Massachusetts, a Z to Apley's A, and she exuded something, an aura, perhaps, a nimbus of substance, something which Walter was very unfamiliar with at the time, this aura being the bearing, the scent, the semblance, the embodiment of qualities of well-bred stock; she was certainly not from New Apley, *no*, that was immediately apparent to Walter, and *yes*, I'm quite aware of this distractingly long lead-in, and multiply compounded and meandering oration, perhaps, more amorphous than a Grateful, Dead, freeform, drug inspired jam, but upon this, more than a nothing of a blind-date interaction, upon her first meeting Walter, at the table for four at Café Lena, ignoring Barry and her classmate, this well-bred and somewhat self-concerned, insolent, self-important, arrogant, imperious, and supercilious c*** simply, off-handedly commented, in a low voice, not low enough to be considered a throw away comment and certainly loud enough to be heard above the mixed cacophony of blended sounds defining the background, directed to Walter, no preamble, just two words, "Nice teeth."

₩KﻗﯼﮒƆƆ¥@#$$%^^&*()()(**%%@#$^+UR$$# $##$

Ignore the above! Symbols, emojis, doodles, cartoon squiggles, no, nothing, they are all less than meaningless; a somewhat poorly conceived and delusive attempt to define an emotional reaction that is not definable or capable of being put into words, ineffable for sure. There is no appropriate symbolism, verbal, written, or drawn for Walter's presumed emotional response to this, while albeit completely observationally correct, this totally devastating, solecistic, and emotionally nuclear comment. Time suspended itself, for a moment at least, perhaps, someone blinked, breathing and blood flow continued, obviously. We refer to Walter's presumed emotional response, since to the world at large, Walter showed no emotion, no acknowledgement of the insult, no counter offer proffered, no comeback in the offing, no witty repartee, *no*, no response whatsoever, nothing detectible at least, any and all reaction to the comments remaining inside of Walter's quite large head. All external neural connections shut down immediately, Walter had excellent survival strategies, perhaps, similar to those of a possum or an ostrich. No response emoted, only a seething internal reaction, maelstrom, perhaps, event horizon lasting for, well, you decide…

A non-reaction was completely to be expected from this Walter. He had no choice, eighteen years and genes dictated his response that night. But perhaps, there were other Walter's, Walter's, who might have proffered more meaningful responses, responses more apropos and direct.

Another Walter, let's forget from where, we have suckled from the teat of multiverses, enough for now me thinks, so let's not pursue that, this other Walter, could have leaped up quite theatrically from his chair, perchance knocking over the table, and spewing its contents, including those four quite dilute, draft beers and the pitcher as well, onto the waxed, far too many times, without being cleaned first, hardwood floor, that floor, all too familiar with beer spills, and experienced with far more than that, and if only that floor could talk and exclaimed (Walter doing the exclaiming, not the floor) as he walked away and prepared to drive solo back to the TIT, he could have responded, "Fuck you, you rich c***," which I, me, the author thinks would have been completely appropriate, and would have been my rejoinder of choice, but upon re-examination, *no*, that never could have happened. Admittedly, however, that response would have provided a quick and quite cinematic ending to the evening! Possibly pleasing all, perhaps, even the rich c***!

Alternatively, moving on, Walter, in a meaningless and empty gesture (Animal House, right?) he could have tossed his fifty-cent draft beer into the face of the unexpecting Louise's, actually, who the fuck knows what she was expecting. After such an aggressive opening line, she should have been prepared for a slew of comebacks. But, *no*, not in her world, in her world, she hurled the insults and there was never a comeback, not even from dear sweet old, likely banker Dad.

Walter never was or would be such a nefarious character, thus, this detailed possibility was never a possibility. Walter often wished otherwise, wished he could be the bad boy, the Bret whoever, to heap disdain and injurious insults onto others. He certainly had the ability to do such and could and did invent such scenarios in his mind. The task was quite simple in fact. However, these both inventive and somewhat obscene continuations of the ongoing play never came to be, they remained, then and to this day, a fantasy scenario, having permanent residence in Walter's getting quite, overly crowded mind.

Taking a higher path, an unlikely option for Walter at that time and place, nevertheless, perhaps, he could have channeled Edmond Rostand's most beloved *Cyrano de Bergerac* and soliloquized a tale most elegant, rivaling Cyrano's eons spanning response to a comment that his nose was somewhat large, his (Cyrano's) response to this insult in part being,

"Ah, no, young sir!

You are too simple. Why, you might have said—

Oh, a great many things? *Mon dieu*, why waste

Your opportunity? For example, thus—

Aggressive: I, sir, if that nose were mine,

I'd have it amputated—on the spot!

Friendly: How do you drink with such a nose?

You ought to have a cup made specially.

Descriptive: This a rock—a crag—a cape—

A cape? say rather, a peninsula!

Inquisitive: What is that receptacle—

A razor-case or a portfolio?

Kindly: Ah, do you love the little birds

So much that when they come and sing to you,

You give them this to perch on?

Insolent: Your chimney is on fire

Perhaps, a more secure, urbane, grandiloquent, or quick-thinking Walter, or perhaps, a fictional Walter could have composed a rebuttal, perchance pleasing Cyrano and it could have started thusly,

"You say nice teeth,

meaning not so,

tis but true,

but be, they so much more.

A misshapen and fearsome sentinel, these but a few enameled soldiers guarding a holy orifice.

Disadvantaged and misaligned they be, *yes*, all true, alas, yet, these enduring pearls, they have seen both pain and war, casting away those unable to see beyond the obvious, letting enter only those of deeper mysteries."

Mysteries such as seeing beyond the obvious, the physical, adjudging none, but accepting all…

And going who knows where, clearly nowhere.

There's more for sure, lots of possibilities, but no, regrettably, or perhaps not, none of these happened."

Louise's comment lacked pathos, sensitivity, poignance, compassion, humanity respect for another fellow being. No ethos, whatsoever.

It, the comment, was defining and demonstrated the moral turpitude of this extremely attractive, privileged, entitled, and insensible young lady; perhaps an attitude adopted by an entire class of seemingly self-nominated entitled individuals. This, however, has always been true, undoubtedly more so today than perhaps back in 1969, and even more appropriate throughout history itself. The small fractional ruling classes have always controlled the masses and the meek and believe me, they, the meek, will never inherit the earth! In her defense, close to post fifty years from the event, easy to expound logic, she was an adolescent, a child, privileged but still, eighteen, at most, she was raised in a perfect world, a world of perfect smiles, of perfect homes, of perfect lawns, of perfect parents, of perfectly orchestrated life's, and even of perfect abortions, and to her, 'nice teeth', it was just two words. But to Walter, it was not just two words, to be more precise, it was two worlds.

Walter's corpse-like response to these two otherworldly words would not be a surprise to anyone who actually knew Walter, at the time, this set was likely limited to two immediate family members.

Of course, he did not acknowledge, ratify, respond to, endorse or deny Louise's two-word opus, really, how could he? He couldn't possibly deny any accurate comment, even one highlighting his easily deprecated teeth, after all, he was, even then and will always be, a scientist, looking at all things from a somewhat distant and aloof, safe scientific perspective. A re-writing of history was the only option available.

Walter quickly retreated to his sanctum sanctorum, a path of avoidance, denial, and refused to accept the reality of the commentary, since if acceptance was given, then acknowledgement of the accuracy, as to the meaning behind those two words would also have to be recognized and perhaps, such acknowledgement would allow for the escape of such malicious information from the sub-conscious and bubble up into the conscious Walter.

Thus, to ensure his survival and sentient continuance, Walter edited away the last thirty or so seconds of reality, he retreated into one of the man rooms in his mind and simply continued to drink his beer and what had just happened, did not happen.

Barry and date, likely, Louise as well, were shocked, shocked into silence, briefly at least, and then, when conversation resumed, it was a non-sequitur.

Barry lamely but compassionately volunteered, "I think I've seen this group before," a distracting, clearly empathetic comment, since, at that time, this never to be remembered group hadn't even taken the stage and it was unlikely that anyone in the coterie of four mismatched souls even knew who was about to take the stage.

An impartial, quantum observer, or perhaps a real observer, an unknown student, from where, sitting at a nearby table, hearing the complete, brief yet poignant conversation, might question whether the Louise insult, regarding Walter's 'orthadontadure' was actually hurled? If it was hurled, was it caught or was it dropped? Perhaps the entire evening, the unabridged Café Lena event was a complete fantasy. Did it occur, was it real, perhaps, it was drug or alcohol related or perhaps, it was a non-drug, a rare but more than once documented, sober group hallucination (somewhat sober, beer was involved after all)? These are all fantastical speculations that have passed through Walter's mind years ago and more recently as well, when he is so inclined as to speculate as to the reality of the events of that more than real evening.

Louise's two-word volley, if one had to comment, seemed to have harmlessly fallen to the floor, no chances taken, thus, no errors recorded, and perhaps, it was to be swept away with the detritus of the night. This previously referenced external observer, hopefully, not influencing the quantum progression of the event might have exclaimed, "What the fuck, wasn't there a dental insult hurled somewhere." But, *no*, Walter's mindly eraser was functioning that night, at least, in the short term, and the evening progressed as most blind or set-up dates do. Meaningless, enhanced, unverifiable, superficial random snippets of conversation.

The artists took the stage, pitchers of beer were consumed (several), sobriety was lost, alcohol, the ultimate mediator, bringing together minds not in harmony (Israel, Palestine, you could learn from this, no let's use a more contemporary reference; Donald and Kim, in fact, let's go Donald and anybody); the sober, conversation ceased, and the evening progressed, this part of the evening meriting no further details. Yada, yada, yada.

Scene switch post-Cafe!

The four (Paul and Walter now occupying the front seats) drove the short distance back from Lena's and deposited the Peugeot in a not quite authorized parking spot. At this time, in 1969, Sagamore was building a new library, and Walter drove quite, in fact, precariously close to, no more than a few feet from a giant pit, that pit, which had been dug and would be the underground library levels, probably several, as books tend to take up a lot of space. Only Barry's acute vision and ability to emit a quite girlishly high-pitched, but quite effective for gaining immediate attention, scream, prevented Walter from blindly driving into that pit. Brakes were applied and the Peugeot, like a well-trained equitation horse, came to an immediate stop. Walter gently pulled back on the reins and his steed backed up a few steps. Both boys peered breathlessly over the dash, Barry, at least, realizing how close they had come to inching over that steep precipice, with who knows what the results would be. Barry was grateful that a preemptive end to his 'who knows what the fuck is going to happen next' date was avoided. "Fuck," was his only underplayed response. Walter somewhat oblivious, was not really consciously aware of what had happened or what could have been. Even stone-cold sober, he was often in his own universe and seemingly unaware, of which universe he actually was in, a lot of important and 'un-important-ness' was missed and at this point in time, he was not stone-cold sober.

Perhaps, if the Peugeot had traversed only a meter or so more of fragile earth and had gently slid down that steep but less than ninety-degree embankment, it would have glided to a safe repose, remaining safe, while there in the future library basement. But this un-played scene, if played out, likely necessitating a pre-emptive termination to the middle grounds of this date would have also necessitated a logistical and financial nightmare for Walter. This not-taken path would have undeniably resulted in a call to his dad and enlisting his help in retrieving the French Lion. But no, this did not happen, the car remained safe, the date would be completed, and from this point A, the French Lion would progress eventually to point B, that point B being a somewhat bloody ending, and that point B occurring two years into Walter's future.

Barry and the number two girl went off somewhere, the tension between the four had abated somewhat, they wanted their alone time. It was agreed Walter and Louise would later meet them in their dorm suite; the dates were suitemates, two of four. Off together on their own and it's hard to believe, it took me quite a while to discard the notion that what the Younger was relating to me was not simply edited or fantasized memories, and now, I do believe his recollection was accurate, and unbelievable as it was, after but a few moments, Walter and Louise off on their twoness, even after all that had happened, most notably the 'Nice Teeth Moment', they forgot what was to be forgotten and seemed to make, albeit temporary, a seemingly real and more than nothing of a connection (and admittedly large amounts of alcohol were involved, and shortly after, during the first part of their walk, Quaaludes but only one each, made a guest appearance. Walter, during this time of reference, was a one or two a day user, a 714 aficionado; a future Walter, the projectile, who flew the windshield of the magical Peugeot, was, after that event, a five or more per day user, medicinal use, mostly used to diminish the lasting and to this day, effects of a chipped C5 vertebrae, head meeting windshield, but ludes or soapers, GABA agonists, were and are, if you can find them, not likely now, far preferred to opioids). This W-L connection resulted in a 'walkabout', together, they walking randomly and serenely about the campus, perhaps, conversing as well, and occasionally, bumping into each other, the game of initiating contact without initiating contact, and as time went on, this contact became more or less permanent and without notice or ado, they were walking as a pair. Bodies leaning against each other, eventually hand contact, walking and talking, hands moist to the touch, hormones slightly increasing body temperature, arms swinging back and forth enthusiastically as a distraction, not quite *Steichschritt* or 'goose-stepping' but a quite humorous picture to be painted. These machinations but a game, a ritual, a destination, 'this train has only one stop.' As it turned out, this foreplay, this rite, was the lead in to an impermanent and superficial bonding of two souls, each with extensive baggage, each with their own unique insecurities, and each striving for perhaps a moment of real, albeit, at least in Louise's case, temporary solace. A tale forever told, an adolescent ritual, pushing each contact a little forward, always forward. One has to be sure motives are in sync, no surprises needed, I think the night was memorable enough already. The conversation, if any, who knows, was incidental, superficial, and long lost. The connection, both were eighteen and in their own and in very different ways, oblivious to the workings of the real world. This was freshman year in college, and after all, college, in no way, can even approximate the real world. College is, or was at the least, the time and place to try the untried, to do the undone, and to move ahead. This feeling, aura, or cloud, the protectionism of college was absolutely true in 1969, today, I'm not so sure!

Whether intentional, accidental, chaotic, Brownian, Louise directed, or guidance via some means not yet known, Walter and Louise ended up next to the magical Peugeot 404.

Without ado, thought, or intention, silently, and unceremoniously, both, Louise and Walter, nebulously entered that magical Peugeot, mutual consensus, no words spoken, it simply happened, just as time passes, seemingly no intent or knowable director. Bucket seats but shift on the column, so only moderately inconvenient, no galumph-ic orchestrations required for the two to assume a somewhat intimate positioning.

It was fall, and it was cool; the breeze was brisk, the leaves had turned color and many were on the ground gyrating, vortexing aimlessly, swirling about like mini-Tasmanian devils, like chipmunks chasing each other's tails. Walter didn't start the car, it wasn't that cool, they rolled down the windows a bit, yes, rolled, windows operated by a hand crank back then, very simple, no battery power required; the air was clean and virginal, you could smell some distant fires, probably, the first fires of the season, these are always welcome, always bringing back fond memories, ostensibly started to warm the nearby homes, but really just to create an energy depleting welcoming ambiance, some of the wood being not properly dried, so you gathered a note of unpleasant smokiness.

It was eerily quiet for a Saturday night at a midsized college campus in 1969. Some muted music from nearby dorms, Walter could make out 'Nights in White Satin' and 'In-a-Gadda-da-Vida', quintessential songs of this era, omnipresent. Some traffic noises, dogs barking, some shrieks of happiness or else, but all noise soon faded to white, it was a world of two.

Louise, not Walter, was the aggressor (and that would be pretty much the story of Walter's entire life, past, present and written and unwritten future); why she took this approach a mystery, especially after her two-word opening oration? Maybe, she simply wanted to test the sinuous, twisted, architecture of Walter's misaligned teeth with her somewhat experienced tongue. It would be an adventure, a new experience, and these were always welcome. In Louise's perfect world, her perfectly lissome tongue had only caressed the surfaces of perfectly orthodontically corrected pearly whites of boys named Chip and Buzz or Winslow III. Tongues were grappling like two John Irving wrestlers, all wet and sweaty, looking for the best position, how to score a point, likely in the 158-pound weight class. There was no conversation, however, points were scored, no takedowns, but some awkwardness. Walter was wearing glasses, Clark Kent-like, fashionable now, but merely serviceable then; the glasses were removed, and then, which direction for the head tilt, left-hand tilt or right-hand tilt, more complicated than need be, but let's remember, Walter was a pre-engineer.

Time passed, nothing unexpected eventuated, experimentation continued, hands and tongues here and there, pick a directional vector and follow it from A to B to

C, unless resistance, then regroup and try a different vector; a scene played out countless times, n > than a lot; played out many times that evening, in fact, and on that campus, without a doubt. The need to connect, the biological imperative, after all reduced to simplistic terms, we (humans) are simply designed to breed and perpetuate the species. We are vessels of propagation, nothing more. We are designed to pass on our own very own special genes, those genes differing only from those of the great apes by perhaps, one percent, but oh, what an important one percent. And if you think about the genetic similarity between siblings and even racially and socially grouped peers, one can wax mystical. But you have to think in reverse. It's not the ten thousand genes you and friend X have in common, it's the 86 genes that are different, that's the story, today and perhaps, tomorrow. Is there a greater, long-term, ineffable mission, than casting your genes? If so, it eludes me, then and now.

I can't speak for Louise, now or then.

Minutes certainly passed, but seemingly nanoseconds went by, Walter eased up and comfortably touched first base and made the turn towards second. Tongues continued to grapple, but another player joined the team, hands, cautiously and not so, moving on their own, *no*, that damn biological imperative was again directing the traffic flow. Each set of hands, one male, one female, knew exactly where they were going. Walter was pretty inexperienced as a batter, had hit a few singles and a few doubles as well, however, third base was uncharted territory. No—this is not a copy-paste error, nor have we seamlessly switched back to the baseball narrative, in this short allegory, we are referring to the baseball sexual allusion here. If you must, Google it!

Louise and Walter were quite relaxed, both had a big lead off second, and they were tempting the pitcher or catcher, to risk a throw and pick them off. Third base was within easy reach. It was magnetic, it had a massive gravitational field, and both were caught within its grasp, slowly it was drawing each away from second base, heedless to their own wishes or desires. The question was who would make the first move, the base was there for the taking, and Walter was slow but was about to take…

Louise, "I'm sorry, I can't"

This hesitant outcry was followed, shortly, thereafter, by some tears, some breathless gasps, and from both, a slight rearrangement of clothing and a return to the accepted driver, passenger seating configuration. Walter's hands returned to the ten and two o'clock position on the steering wheel, that position we all learn in driving class as being the most safe and secure place for your hands when in a car, regardless of its state of motion. This unexpected, emotional reaction from Louise took Walter completely off-guard. He was expecting some resistance or perhaps an outright rejection of the events ongoing, but this, this was a surprise. And part of the surprise was the seemingly genuine effluence of real emotions and feeling. In his mind, although they had only made a superficial contact, all this was just adolescent play, this was a cold bitch, a girl with little concern for anything but herself, and her immediate gratification and more likely, her current status, not Facebook status, that's almost forty years down the road.

Louise continued and there was no hesitation now, she seemed to be on a roll, letting whatever she had to say be free, rapid fire, staccato-like explosions, barely a breath taken between the start and finish of her revelation. "I had an abortion six months ago, it was near the end of the school year, I homeschooled the last few months, when it began to show. I can't fucking believe it was the first and only time I had sex. It wasn't planned and I don' think either one of us expected it."

Walter sat there quietly, he was actually focused on this short tale, just wondering where this was heading and perhaps, why she was opening up to Mr. Nice Teeth. "Both, Robert and I, had been drinking, not a lot, he had taken some vodka from his Dad's office bar, he did that quite often, we drank before, but just a bit, you know just to get a little buzz but I don't think we were drunk."

Legally, perhaps not, behaviorally, most definitely. "And then, he just did it! I don't even remember what happened it was so quick. He was my high school boyfriend from forever, he was my first kiss and our families vacationed together on the Vineyard since the early fifties. We were sitting there just like this, in his dad's Porsche and it just happened (Walter drifted a bit, made a mental note, Porsche!). I had to tell my parents when I knew for sure and they insisted on the abortion. I let them have complete control over the decision and why not, any future guilt, it's theirs, not mine. I didn't even tell Robert, we stopped seeing each other after that night but I'm sure he knew about it (about both, in fact, the pregnancy and the abortion). I think everybody in town knew (knows) about it, even though no one would considered mentioning it to my *oh* so important dad. He still thinks it's a secret, he's delusional for sure! I was so glad to leave Newton and come to Sagamore. I am never going back to Newton."

Louise finally takes a deep breath, several, in fact, as if a diver resurfacing after far too long a descent. Her tale, her oration, the first of what will become two on this long October eve, now, complete.

A decidedly real silence, a break in this theatre or perhaps game, and suddenly, the umpire steps out, actually, literally leaps out from behind, home plate and calls time; he takes his mask off and calls for a meeting at the pitcher's mound. Both managers exit the dugout and walk to the mound. Lots of talking. The infielders leave their positions and also gather at the mound, more opinion is needed; it may come down to a vote. After a somewhat protracted discussion, a lot of physicality and animation by all involved, the game is called, it is over, no further play, no runs have scored, and it will be recorded as thus. Walter and Louise go back to their respective benches.

********

Up until this very moment, this pause in the narrative, this page you are now reading, and repeating this just to make sure you get this, it's important, up until this very moment, the only fictional elements of this purportedly fictional TIT-Sagamore College interaction are the names of the actors in this drama; proper nouns, places, things, etc., as well, at least some.

And actually, Louise is not a fictional name, but certainly a made-up name, it might be real, since Walter, the author as well, obviously, has no fucking idea as to what the real name of this fictional girl was, but we are both almost certain it is not Louise and she did not hail from Newton! And by the way, do fictional girls have a real name, or a place of residence, answer me that? Believe me, both, Walter and I, have tried to recreate that name, even tried the A to Z thing, it simply does not work. Walter's mindly eraser was working quite well that Sagamore night.

Walter, Barry, and Vinny are far more real than one might hope, they are real for sure, although they might be more than one person, a composite actually, certainly. Vinny seems bigger than life, how could a single person encompass all that was Vinny. I can still see his completely eviscerating grin. Vinny, well, Vinny is Vinny, but he is no Vinny I ever had the pleasure of meeting. I hope he is as happy now as when I didn't know him.

It's also entirely possible that Barry has been cobbled together from Josh and Sol, or Howie and Hymie, who knows, maybe he was a composite of my high school comrades, all high achieving Jews, and the only bodies in a high school class of more than two hundred willing to add me, younger Walter that is, to their club. And Ami, well I'm sure Ami knows exactly who he is, or is not, and if he does, then kudos to a more real than real Ami.

As to the fiction or reality of this evening, many, most in fact, of the events described, unless disclaimed beforehand, and forthcoming events (those about to be detailed and in other universes included as well) all happened; they were real, mostly, as real as the bond between carbon and hydrogen, that bond arguably forming the basis for all life as we know it or maybe not, perhaps, this reality, our perceived reality, is just a virtual simulation.

Whether fact or fiction, real or imagined, these events, on this transcendental Sagamore eve, played a more than a real and major role in the present, past, and future development of Walter's psyche. Ignore the publisher's disclaimer, read the 'Pale King'! This was real…arguably!

However, while this sexually charged episodic prelude and the herein described events may be real and singular, the denouement to this narrative is not singular, it has a myriad of Feynman variations. Some being real and others real only in Walter's mind, and in the now, we just have to take Walter's word for what was the real, real.

Thus, in this universe, in the past world, according to Walter, the one I'm sure we all exist in, this is what actually happened (arguably).


## No Stop:

Before we disclose the real finale, let's first look, just for fun, at what happened in other realities, the multiverses we have no access to, those realities made up in Walter's mind.

Version 1: In fact, the only alternate version we will describe.

For days, weeks, perhaps years, after this disturbing and traumatic event occurred, Walter relived and revised every minute of that evening. Each revision had subtle changes and each a slightly different ending. However, in many, most, in fact, of these revised editions, Walter consoled Louise, talked her down from the edge so to speak, they connected, he imparted upon her sage advice and they went back to the dorm suite; they hugged, they kissed, fondly not sexually, and they each went off their own separate ways. As both, Walter (v1) and Louise (v1), continued their distinct journeys through life, they maintained contact, communicated with each other, and years later, obviously, after it came to life, they became Facebook friends! Louise eventually had children, before Facebook, of course, if you are at all concerned with the timeline and named her second son Walter.

I knew the 1969 Walter (obviously), and few others did, perhaps far fewer than you might imagine, or then again, maybe not. It seems likely he, Walter, made an effort, perhaps consciously, perhaps not, to remain an enigma.

Current time, narrative future Walter, and the author, without a doubt, both know that today's Walter, minus fifty years or so, could, in no way, have been a part to such a platitudinous ending to such a tale. It's unlikely he even pondered such ideas back in 1969 but somehow, he must have, thus, this narrative. Self-delusion is delightful, I think I am repeating but that point is worth repeating!

There are so many fucking things wrong with the fantasy scenario detailed above, it's an onerous undertaking to decide where to start to refute such prattle; but I can factually say, knowing Walter quite well, that the aforementioned fantasized scenario is pure hokum, hooey, poppy-cock, wampum, guff, bosh, bunkum, malarkey, gibberish, and clap-trap; it's so far from any possible Walter truth that it's the perfect antipodean of what really happened.

The pure fantastical projection that young Walter could and would behave in such an adult, mature, and caring manner is patently absurd for several reasons, some not known to Walter at the time, and perhaps, today as well, but nevertheless true, these facts concerning his ideology or more aptly put his particular weltanschauung.

At the time of the dental insult, the precipitating event in this ongoing drama, young Walter didn't have the life experience, the confidence, the self-assurance, self-direction, poise, plunk, spunk, *élan*, or heroism to follow that road; that road of compassion, of being a mentor, of showing empathy and pathos; of proving in fact that he was perfectly dissimilar from the arrogant, albeit elegant *cunt*, whom had just shaken Walter's shoddily constructed (house of cards built) ego to its very foundation.

No Walter had no choice, he was programmed, genetically designed, his brain microstructures had already been hardwired and pre-determined to take another road; this road being that of minimizing the damage to self (the damage sustained earlier that evening) as well as the short and long-term damage to his physical being and his subconscious self.

Walter's next actions were only shadow actions, only shadow options were available, as he was then, only a shadow person. He contemplated and fantasized many different real responses, perhaps, even the one above, but also others more Walter-like, nonviable possibilities, those such as revenge, retribution, payback, and getting even.

# But is there free will, really,

## and does this question have a

### black and white answer?

This may be a question

answered in the gray!

Walter had so many choices as what to do next, but did he really? Were they not already predetermined by some eighteen years of experience and the genes passed onto him from mom and dad.

It's almost certain, the ending to this short tale was the only possible ending in this world at that place and time. And this is the ending, the ending that did really happen. It is not a fantasy ending and this is not an alternate universe ending, this is the actual real-world happenings. The end to this story, this Walter nonfiction, this permanently recorded 'memory', and as best we can detail on these pages, was an ending not written by Walter's conscious direction, but more likely by a subconscious force, and that direction being dictated not by mind or thought but simply by our biological imperative.

So, Walter, rather than to venture, a supportive, emphatic, and mentoring position and risk possible and further rejection (in other words, version one and in fact, the only alternative version we will detail), Walter opted for plan B, or perhaps, it was A, all along.

For the sake of getting us back on point in this digression from a digression, perhaps, another digression needed for accuracy sake, a very terse Series 2, episode 1 recap of Season 1 follows, "We are awaiting Walter's response to the emotion filled confession of Louise."

A predictable, short, and absolute silence followed, it was the classic awkward silence, it was deafening within the confines of the Peugeot, windows, now fogging over, and visibility completely impaired, but no visibility was needed for the ending of this tale to play out.

Walter, after a moment of pause, not a thoughtful pause, simply a pause, simply, and not at all forcefully, as none was required, decided to reengage with Louise and follow direction from that damn but *oh* so blessed biological imperative. When the ballgame was halted, they both had good leads off second, so why not retake the field and resume play where it has left off. Louise seemed quite happy to do so, and via an ethereal or perhaps biological force, both participants re-engaged and continued to follow directions, from who knows where and simply concluded what was fated from the moment they both entered the magical world of the French Lion. Louise, in fact, was considerably more enthusiastic than Walter, who, it seemed, was simply following stage directions that he knew not thereof. They continued their adventures, seemingly both parties, somewhat engaged and 'in the moment.'

As to the conclusion of the game, I think for proprietary's sake, we have detailed more than enough of this short encounter than appropriate already, let's leave the balance of that evening, regarding the continuing events in that slightly steamy French Lion, firmly in the real and fictional past, where these events began, where they now exist, and where they belong, and forever remain, except adding one more detail, and to emphatically state for the record, 'third base was taken that evening, both parties being accorded the base, both enthusiastically so, but not credited as a stolen base, simply recorded as defensive indifference.'

*******

## Scene Change

Sagamore College Freshman Dorm, dorm name unknown, suite number, also, not known.

Louise and Walter, after their somewhat, emotion filled and hastily completed tryst, made their way back to the dorm with no name, the pre-arranged after date meeting place. Barry was waiting for them, there in the lobby, seemingly guarding the entrance, Centurion duties, and his date nowhere to be seen, obviously, she made an early exit. Barry was half asleep, slouching a bit; however, being that slouching was his default posture, it was difficult to adjudge if he was, in fact, half asleep or simply passing time. Nevertheless, upon seeing Louise and Walter, walking together, not touching, not talking, just striding in syncopation, physical proximity but cerebral and ideological antipodes, and the two abstractly gravitating towards the stairs leading to the suitemates suite on the second floor, Barry effortlessly levitated himself from the burgundy red bean-bag chair which he had obviously repositioned to strategically keep guard of the dorm entrance, and like a Giraffe on the plains of the Serengeti, he fully stretched out his six-foot three frame. The transition was impressive and caught the attention of, both, Louise and Walter.

Barry reached out, "How's it going?" (BTW, 'reached out' definitely an anachronism, never used until long after this drama played out).

There was no response from either of the 'trustees', they barely acknowledged him, Louise, in fact, did not, she ignored such banality, easy to do, as she had the 'breeding thing' going for her. Walter nodded, acknowledged Barry's existence and they, Walter and Louise, continued their distracted perambulation to places known. While he had only known her, and he really had not known her in any sense or meaning of the word, and this not knowing, being but for a few short hours, Walter, nevertheless, believed he had completely fathomed all aspects of Louise's psyche and knew exactly what she was thinking. Or, at least, in his completely blind and unrealistically, delusional self-assuredness, he thought so.

Barry fell in behind them, the group, now, a threesome, still no words spoken, he was a happy soldier and after all, he did need a ride home, back to the Tute. He, maintaining contact, was important as he quickly needed to determine if a return trip to the TIT was in the offing or just a long night in the lobby of the dorm, that likely being the case, if the extremely implausible outcome of Walter's evening was a sleepover at SC. If, in fact, that was the play, hastily securing alternative transportation back to the Tute was his prime directive. These (logistic problems) happened quite often; in fact, whenever a group of males went on the hunt and travelled to the village of eligible females, it was inevitable that if the alpha-male scored and he likely, also, being the wheel man, the remainder of the tribe was forced to spend the night in the bushes, fending off packs of wild animals and hoping just to survive till the next morning. Been going on for millennia!

Walter oft went on these hunting expeditions, mostly with the aforementioned questionable but definitely alpha-roommate Vinny, who was more often than not successful at finding accommodations for the night, thus, being a quick learner, Walter, in no time at all, succeeded in learning how to survive the night on his own. Barry's survival skills, highly questionable.

All three heroes of this odyssey, Barry, assuming the role of rear guard, trudged up the sixteen steps, two sets of eight, reversing direction at midpoint, poured concrete, no carpeting, and unlike the Nathan Hall stairwells, there was barely a smell of puke or urine, and this group of three, quietly and all seemingly, enjoying a drug and alcohol induced mellowness, exited the stairwell on level two. The three made a sharp right turn, passed a utility closet, smelling of what utility closets smell of, and then making another right, all three cast members entered the common area of the second-floor dorm suite and although it was well past midnight on this eventful eve, quite a large small crowd was gathered. The group in its entirety, had partitioned into many sub-groups and was enjoying the pleasure of nothingness, meaningless, temporal interactions, completely unaware of the unpredicted vector this evening was soon to take.

The common area was not large, perhaps, twenty by thirty feet, but on this particular Saturday night, that space accommodated perhaps forty or more students, roughly equal numbers of males and females. This student density, likely a code violation and important to people concerned with such trivial matters as maximal room occupancy, but few others, was not unusual, especially true for any (perhaps all) Friday or Saturday nights, while classes were in session. Often dates started and ended here. The lounge became an ad hoc meeting place, staging area, more often filled with outsiders than with the Sagamore coeds. There was a single, doorless, double-wide entrance; inside were several gray non-descript fabric encased, slightly disquieting sofas symmetrically positioned, opposed to each other. They looked much cleaner and had significantly less damage than those scattered throughout the TIT freshman dorms. A few chairs opposed the pair, and a coffee table was positioned between the two sofas, upon which, randomly existed, just here and there, a gallimaufry of alcoholic beverages, some loose marijuana, mostly seeds and stems, and a few poorly rolled joints, an assortment of pills (Walter quickly ascertained no 714s), postage stamps (certainly *not* U.S. Postal Service regulation) , red plastic cups, some empty, some filled with a slightly disgusting amber liquid, and others, clearly providing a service as mini fire extinguishers as they contained the remnants of assorted small white cylindrical torches, but none holding coffee or a fact-simile thereof, something which Walter was desperately in search of. On a primitive TV stand, composed of six standard fare cinder blocks, (3-2-1 orientation), was a seventeen inch, with rabbit ear, antennae Zenith TV. Oddly, the TV caught Walter's attention and, in a time-free distraction, he momentarily fixated upon that being-less piece of technology. As if caught in a time-loop, he did several double-takes, each time he focused on the TV, as expected it was lifeless, in fact, Walter noticed it was not plugged in. However, he was quite certain that each time he looked away that 17" Zenith came to life. Walter took several deep breathes and several moments to compose himself and decided to ignore this modest hallucination. After all, a variety and not a low concentration thereof of foreign substances were coursing through his circulatory system, not a surprise, as this was a weekend evening.

Walter recognized one or two TIT classmates. He immediately noticed Ami (his real name was Ahmed), a larger than life character, who resided only a few rooms down from Walter on the second floor of Nathan Hall. Ami was of some African L descent (Lebanon, Libya, Lesotho, Walter had forgotten which) and he looked it. Walter remembered Ami owed him five dollars, not important, well, it was important, but Walter knew that money was lost! Ami came from a wealthy, perhaps, titled family and also looked it, a regal look to him. A certain 'bearing', a gravitas were the words that came to mind. Ami was quite dark and had gargantuan features, nose, ears, brow, and lips. However, these caricatures of anatomy worked on Ami. He was tall and broad shouldered, not 'ripped', perhaps, in good cardiovascular shape, no one was 'ripped' back then, perhaps, gymnasts and wrestlers, but certainly not TIT students. He was not handsome but interesting. His appeal was his ebullience and his positive and captivating, enthralling, magnetizing, and rapturing presence. Wherever Ami was, he was in-charge of the room. People and groups just naturally gravitated towards him. He was magnetic, of opposite charge from the masses, *no*, it was more than that, it was as if he was flypaper and you were the fly. Once within his sphere of influence, you couldn't or simply didn't have the inertial impetus to leave. Walter felt small in so many ways in his presence. Not just physical size, *yes*, Walter was a good four inches and thirty pounds smaller than Ami, but, *no*, that wasn't it. Then and even now, Walter really couldn't/can't explain the whats and whys. It just was! Walter did, however, luxuriate, and he, reliving key parts of the forthcoming revelation, quite frequently, wasting hours daily, in the knowledge that every Tuesday morning, when there were no engineering recitations or lab sessions, essentially, free time or for most study time, Walter and Ami would perambulate down to the '78' gym and spend a few hours sweating it out over half a dozen or so games of handball. Walter would always win, 4-2, 5-1, rarely, 6-0. Rarely 6-0 by intent. Walter never had the killer instinct, it's a fairly common trait. Why win 6-0, risk embarrassing your opponent and perhaps, eliminate the possibility of future matches and victories. No 5-1 or 4-2 was good enough. Ami, knowing he could win one or two games, would be certain that things would change and next week, the results would be different and he would be the victor. After all, the balance of the universe was in his favor, he was Ami and Walter, well, he was just Walter.

Handball was a game unfamiliar to Walter until he matriculated at the TIT, probably wasn't aware of its existence until about twenty-four hours after his campus arrival. To Ami, however, handball was his baseball, his great L country pastime, both in L and later on the streets of Miami. Any open space with a concrete wall or, in fact, any wall that was somewhat solid would do. Chalk a few lines on the wall and configure a rectangle on the surrounding grounds, hopefully, asphalt, the exact dimensions not really mattering, and voila, an instant handball court. A ball, who cares if it is regulation or not, and no gloves needed, hands quickly toughened to the impact of that rubber ball being slapped again and again, against that enduring and unforgiving adversary, the wall. Side walls would be welcome but not really necessary.

Miami was where Ami's family had emigrated to, or as he often commented, only half-jokingly, escaped to, no further details forthcoming. Ami was always looking over his shoulder, as if someone, someone who perhaps, shouldn't be there, that someone was there. Other than this quite frequent, paranoid behavior, Ami seemed completely happy. Ami would spend the last several years of high school in that sun-drenched city, a city welcoming pretty much any and all immigrants, regardless of port of origin. Upon high school graduation, Ami shipping off to the TIT, where he would pursue and be granted an engineering degree (B.S.), and attend graduate school, not the TIT however. Walter lost contact with Ami shortly after freshman year, the handball games ended, Ami joined a prestigious jock fraternity, in spite of he not being such, and Walter was, as you might have guessed, an independent; a term given to someone not inclined to join or be considered acceptable fodder for any fraternity, including the nerd fraternity, thus, Walter being oil and Ami being water, beyond that freshman year and their more than a few games of handball, they were completely immiscible and never beyond that freshman year would a W-A handball game occur. On the upside, Walter did retire undefeated!

With a passing interest and gathering info from second and third-hand sources, Walter did casually follow Ami's future, at the TIT and beyond (would have been a fuckload easier if Facebook existed back then) and Walter, surprisingly, perhaps not, learned that Ami, after completing his undergraduate and graduate degrees, headed back to the L country, and was apparently put in charge of some government (i.e., U.S. or Russia funded) technical arms or other technology development program (only author speculation here regarding the nature of the project and its funding) and was doing just fine. Walter could not determine whether Ami continued his losing ways in handball after freshman year.

Within the first month at the TIT, Walter likely had spent close to fifty hours playing the game, more often than not on his own, playing against that relentless wall, no opponent necessary. No chance of losing or perhaps, you always lost, how do you beat a wall after all? It was the perfect Walter experience. These solo games, and the ones played against Ami as well, were played on the very isolated squash courts, re-purposed for handball and years later for racquetball, these courts located on the basement level of the '78' gym. Squash, after all, was and perhaps is a dying sport, a game of the elite, although new information does suggest it may be on the rise, perhaps, the Millennials will spearhead its reemergence. The '78' gym was an impressive brick structure, protecting the northeast corner of the Van der Waals Football Field. At the time, it was the main and only athletic facility on campus. The TIT had an imposing, nationally ranked synchronized skating team and of course, they had their own private facility 'The Skatehouse.' Included were state-of-the-art training rooms, PT facilities and much more, however, it only served the elite skaters; it was also quite far away at the opposite end of the campus. The '78' gym was not built in 1878, which one might initially assume, it was pretty old but quite a few years younger, actually, being built in 1921. It was called the '78'gym that name coming into existence because of the charitable contributions of several members of the class of '78', (that's 1878), now, that makes sense.

These solitary handball games, simply being played against the wall were not really games, how could they be? Walter was playing a wall after all; what these simple practices were, were experiences, experiences far more important than a simple game. These sessions were hugely important to the Walter psyche. Walter was isolated, the harsh world outside the confines of this small rectangular cuboid did not exist. To Walter this small universe was his alone, a world in which he was in complete control, wherein Walter's mind unfettered by an intrusive and disturbing reality was sovereign; ball, angles, velocity, no external distractions; a far better than drug experience. No judgments, no denigrations, no failures, no expectations, real or otherwise. No other people. However, the result of these inwardly focused and singular Walter times, was within no time at all, Walter became a student of and excelled quite nicely in the game of handball. After all, all it was, was math! Be at the right place at the right time. Simply, angles and 3D geometry. Beating Ami at 'his own game' was one of the few pleasures Walter relied on. It happened every Tuesday on a regular basis, fifteen weeks at a time, the length of each semester at the TIT at that time. It, these meaningless victories were, for Walter, not meaningless, but a guerdon to grasp and tightly hold onto; this guerdon to provide a barrier and fortress, fending off the misery of his somewhat oppressive existence. This misery lasting more than days, extending onto weeks and months. This misery, one that Walter was fighting and losing an uphill battle with, was the completely real and undeniable realization, becoming stronger each day, the realization being he was not special; he was just an average Tute freshman. This averageness, a far different reality from the one that had been programmed into him by his loving and overly supportive parents for the previous eighteen years; it was unlikely Walter would be able to live up to their or his expectations.

Ami, at least, as Walter saw him, was just a loving person. It seemed, to Walter, he loved just about everything. He loved the school, and he loved Nathan Hall. He loved 8 a.m. chemistry lab sessions, he loved handball, and based upon his demeanor and reactions, it's possible he loved losing to Walter. He, seemingly and who can possibly fathom why, even loved the somewhat squalid and fetid city of Troy. Why he was so enraptured by his life in Troy, which often has been referred to as 'Troilet', is not known? Perhaps, it, Troy, was better than L or the streets of Miami or perhaps, Ami was simply the quintessential, archetypal optimist, only seeing the good, which at the time, perhaps, today as well, completely eluded Water's perspective.

He immediately saw Walter and called him over.

"Hey man, you look wasted."

A typical opening commentary, more oft correct than not in the late 1960s, perhaps, today as well.

"Nah, some beer, was at Lena's, did a soaper, just one, pretty tame now."

"She yours?" Ami orienting his head in the direction of Louise, who was having quite an animated discussion with several suitemates, and as time passed, in fact, in real time, the all-female circle surrounding her was rapidly expanding, as if a wildfire consuming overly dry tinder.

"Blind date, not terrible."

"Jamaica?"[26]

Walter was not sure how to answer this. He never had sex, he wasn't sure what this reference actually implied, was coitus necessary or did reaching any one of the bases count; and he being a somewhat inexperienced, nerdy, flavorless, and uninspiring scientist, he didn't want to give the wrong answer, especially to Ami. Third base was third base after all and it was his first MLB triple.

Thankfully, Walter never got the chance to answer that weighty inquiry. While his mouth began to open and initiate some word formation, and, likely Walter not knowing what, but certainly caring what he would spew forth to Ami, his verbalized thoughts and pre-words were preempted by the indignant and righteous not quite shrieking, but not completely composed and somewhat loud, broadcasting of just four words, twice as many, and different from the words that opened this drama, far different, in fact. And, those words, simply ejaculated into the air, by Louise, of course, by Louise, she seemingly, now less composed than a few minutes past, but still, somewhat composed and at the same time, seemingly out of control, and those, now, four words broadcast to those within auditory range, were the not so simple words

---

[26] Finally back to footnotes, we seem to have momentarily ignored these important expansions of the narrative, this comment Jamaica, refers to a Led Zeppelin song, wherein the phonetics of the pronunciation of the tiny island of Jamaica approximates the phrase 'did you make her'; a not so polite way of saying did you have sex with your date.

No symbols, letters, emojis this time; nonsense squiggles will not convey the aura, the emotions, nor the thoughts of insanity. We have tried, more than once and it just can't be done. Some of us might be able to pull from our own life experiences and grasp a flavor of the life force that, now, permeated this room a force which I will not attempt to reduce to words

It was only a little after 12:30 a.m., quite early for a campus weekend, pretty much any campus. The room of forty plus or so, other than the Louise caucus, had separated into small groups mostly twos, threes, and fours, numerous conversations were ongoing, most about music, sex, or drugs, what else, the drug conversations were based upon actual experience and knowledge (the sex dialogs mostly theoretical). TIT freshman tended to be excellent chemists, most had experimented in the organic chemistry lab in Westley Hall, usually without but sometimes with their proctor's knowledge and help, as to what extraction process would result in the most potent concoction, that extract providing the most distanced and temporal relief from the realities of the TIT. The marijuana available in the late 1960s, especially true for Troy, NY, was pretty tame, low-quality pot with a pitiful concentration of tetrahydrocannabinol. In all likelihood, most of the pot available to TIT freshman was locally grown. For those who now know or those who knew Walter, they will confirm that he often questioned whether the highs he and his friends, peers, and temporal acquaintances experienced were due to the tetrahydrocannabinol content, the active hallucinogen in marijuana, or simply due to anoxia, a smoke induced reduction of oxygen availability within the brain. So considerable time and effort was undertaken, after regular working hours, in these laboratories, wherein these slightly less than social, pubescent future leaders of science and technology would spend hours optimizing extraction processes, so, eventually, whatever end product they created; paste, resin, crystals, gum, etc., this product would be considerably enriched in the *oh* so desired tetrahydrocannabinol. Less smoke more drug a win-win for all.

However, these meaningless and time facilitating discussions ceased, as all within that mini-verse suddenly realized that something important, or at least entertaining, was being vocalized by a very attractive, somewhat tall, blond, and ethically blind young lady, who was now the center of attention of that small universe.

She repeated herself, perhaps for emphasis, or perhaps, some in the room had missed her opening

*"I was just raped."*

Peripheral conversations and all things verbal abruptly terminated as *all* attention shifted to the 'blackhole' steadily growing in the far corner of the room. A few conversations, to the embarrassment of the assembled, continued unaware of the instant silence, and those conversations, private or not, were loudly broadcast to all, continuing, as the growing quiet brusquely settled on the room, as quickly as a putt left just a few turns short of the cup; a sudden and unexpected quiet and suddenly, your private words become part of collective society. Have I just defined social media?

Ears are fixed, but indeed, in this room, at the commencement of Louise's oration, those ears did, in fact, rotate, as all those gathered in the small, over-crowded lounge positioned themselves or their ears to hear the continuation of Lady Louise's diatribe. She was no longer talking to her immediate group but now had complete control of the lounge itself.

Her completely fallacious (no intended reference to fellatio, well, perhaps, just a tad, maybe even more than a tad), salacious, and fantastical narrative enraptured the group of forty or so pharmaceutically diminished coeds, almost all, in fact all, being TIT 'co's' and Sagamore 'ed's' or perhaps the opposite. Is a 'co' male and the 'ed' female? Does anybody know or care? The oracle has no answer.

The speaker's corner was secured, she had full attention of all, and assured with this knowledge, continued her sophistic description of an event that did not happen nor could have ever happened with Walter as a central character.

No longer simply Louise, she had become Mother Earth, the center of the Ptolemian Universe, and within that newly created universe, she embodied every feminine heroine of times; past, present, and future. She was Cleopatra, Clara Barton, Jenny Fields, Helen of Troy, she was Sappho, Sacagawea, Madam Curie, and she was Rosa and Sandra Day. Lackies brought her Saratoga Spring water to keep her lips from drying, voice from cracking and to protect her delicate vocal chords, those heavenly structures, which quite recently had been in close proximity to little Walter, and we will state again at her own volition, from drying out, as she orated and proceeded forth. In hyperbolized and beyond embellished detail, she described her date with this hideous man, a deceiver, a Judas, a

Cyrano with lapidarian features, an Ignatius, a genius of deceit, Machiavellian, a Don Juan, a seducer, a Lothario, all, in fact, embodied into the non-descript five-foot eight frame of a TIT freshman, now with fenestration gaping, gnarled dentins exposed to all, listening in horror and to some degree, admiration, to the tale being woven on the fabric of a Sagamore College Saturday night.

Real and meaningful details and truths were left out, fantasy prevailed, but of course, to weave an interesting tapestry, the substance must be altered to suit the expectations of the intended audience. Truth can be exceedingly dull, as well as painful.

Louise described in somber (and excruciating detail, perhaps, like an unpublished novelist), her blind date with a foul toothed and foul spirited TIT freshman. He plied her with drugs, isolated her from the herd, and against physical and verbal admonitions, had his way with her. Her monologue was, in fact, a super Nova, a brilliantine's extravagance, a blinding illumination compared to this trite, hastily constructed and somewhat, placid memory reconstruction.

The entire oration was but a few minutes or so, but time suspended itself in Walter's mind and the inquisition seemed endless. Newton was wrong, Einstein was correct; time, time is definitely not a constant and is quite flexible. Time is silly putty, it can be compressed into almost nothingness, reduced to an infinitesimal size with an infinite density or drawn out almost infinitely into a never-ending string, these manipulations all but ensuring that joy is ephemeral, barely a fleeting moment, and torment is not such, but enduring and everlasting. She, Louise, finished her elegant diatribe, pointed to Walter as the offender and Louise, with what I can only describe as her crew (a genuine anachronism here) left the lounge for destinations unknown. The scene ended, and the stage vacated; that forever moment was the last time Walter would ever see or communicate, in any form, written, oral, spiritual, or transcendentally, with that fictional but far more than real Louise. So much for being future Facebook friends!

An interminable and turbulent silence ensures-duration unknown.

********

# Part 5

## Post-Rape and Back to the Tute

New scene, actors return to the stage, audience re-engages. Those remaining, present, and accounted for, all shocked, astounded, thunderstruck, floored, blown away, both, the players and the spectators alike. But only momentarily, the shroud of astonishment lifting, slowly, like the curtain rising on a new production, this production already in the third act! The tenuous quiet continues, but some hushed conversations are springing forth, and soon, all realize that indeed a 'What the fuck moment' had just happened, no doubt about that; it was equal parts real, surreal, unreal, all of the above, and so much more. In the now, the lounge was largely, actually, entirely filled with TIT students; of course, these were all male. The female half of the group, Louise Disciples, thankfully, had all left, a mass exodus, biblical proportions. Those now remaining, the future engineers and scientists whose dates, prospective dates, anticipated bedmates, or plus ones, had fled the scene, being part of the growing but thankfully, ephemeral and fugacious Louise movement were mindlessly milling about, cow-like (perhaps, the earlier Labrador reference also applies), completely taken aback and out of their comfort zone, if, in fact, any of these slightly ingenuous and jejune young men had a comfort zone. An aerial view would have shown perhaps six or seven partite groups, the largest group bonded quite tightly to Ami; Walter among the attracted clumps of matter. Most were being blissfully distracted and fighting a tug-of-war battle between the fascinating happenings *du moment* and the magnetic, gravitational, electromagnetic force, whatever (many options they were engineers after all) pull of the drug or intoxicant these fledgling engineers chose to be their soulmate for the evening, and this chemical soul-mate trying to seduce, to desperately extract, individually and collectively, each and all, away from this potentially histrionic drama, awaiting them and needing to be completed.

The lounge was quiet, eerily so, any continuing conversation was hushed, heads drawn close together, mostly one on ones; music, drifting in only from afar, multiple sources all merging into whitish noise. There was still quite a small large group, obviously smaller than the large small group gathered somewhat earlier; the remaining participants in tonight's drama were attempting to wrap their quite large, intoxicated heads around the happenings of just a moment passed. Still stunned, no tests had or could have prepared these partial adults for the events of this evening, but how to react? Unabridged silence was to be expected, and this, the default setting, since most of these engineers were as far from alpha males as zeta is from alpha. All these reticent, quite bright men boys, were normally non-participants, withheld comments, rarely ventured an opinion, unless directly queried, so how could they possibly respond to such an oration? It was a world they had not lived in. No rejoinders were in the offing (a robotic 'does not compute' was flying about). This hemorrhagic silence, how long could it go on, an entropy thing, right? The dynamics of the room were not favorable for this to continue much longer. And, of course, it did not continue much longer, and of course, the silence was broken, and of course, who was it that broke that silence, and again of course, it was no one but of course flypaper Ami, Ami to the rescue. That was the past and this is clearly not, it's the present time, and now, in this present time, almost fifty years subsequent to this transformative event, and after far too many hours wasted reflecting upon this event, mostly late at night when insomnia, and on occasion, in fact, more than on just a few occasions, alcohol as well, takes control of all logical thought, and when only emotion and insecurities dictate our thoughts, Walter has come to the conclusion that in all and any of the Everett[27] multiverses, this outcome, Ami taking control of the room and dictating the events of the remainder of the evening was the only possible next step and outcome. Alternative possibilities are not and were not and will not be possible.

Ami's next move, the breaking of the strained silence, was simply a comment thrown out into the quietude of the

---

[27] Hugh Everett is, arguably, credited with the first reasonably documented multiverse hypothesis, proffered in 1954 during a drinking session with a number of grad students at Princeton. The history of this event suggests he was apparently drinking sherry. This revelation pre-dates the many LSD, mushroom, and other hallucinogen inspired cosmological brainstorms during the 1960s, 1970s and thereafter, wherein, so many variations of the multiverse idea were explored with vigorous enthusiasm.

assembly, competing with the random noises from adjacent rooms, a distinct and quite annoying ticking (the contracting and expanding of the metal fins, obviously from the electrical heating units, strategically placed along the base of the walls of the lounge), and the ubiquitous Iron Butterfly standing out a bit from the white noise musical background. And Ami's comment, while not spoken very loudly, nonetheless, eclipsed all other sounds, commanded the attention of all, and that comment was, "Fuck dude[28], was that really you?"

It seems this entire drama has been defined by twelve simple words, two spoken to initiate this adventure, four more of an accusatory note, and now six more to move this adventure to its logical, or least a, conclusion.

Walter was slightly taken aback, more than slightly, actually, he was utterly and completely befuddled by this Ami comment, as it had distinct undertones of approval, impossible, but yes. The upsetting beginnings of this transcendental evening at Lena's, and the subsequent events were already quite beyond any reasonable or imagined expectations Walter contemplated. In Walter's mind, it was going to be another typical Saturday night, first unrealistic anticipations of what was to come, next a somewhat stilted

---

[28] The author cannot be sure whether dude was actually used. Although the term dude was coined in the 1800s to describe a dandy or an extravagant individual, modern usage originated as many things do in California, in the surfing community. It was likely in use nationwide in the late 1960s, but the author acknowledges that this may be an anachronism for the TIT community (or perhaps Walter's TIT community) in 1969.

attempt at a connection, and finally, the inevitable, complete, and utter rejection; however, this continuing drama was reaching into depths of alien origin, most definitely otherworldly.

Ami's simple, succinct, and pointed few words, that was Ami, it was how he was wired, it was in his DNA, i.e., his biological hardware or perhaps software, nonetheless, those few words here provided stage direction for this continuing drama. Words were Ami's currency, why spend more than you must. Nonetheless, this breviloquent comment begged the question, was Nathan Hall Walter, *the* Walter we all know and ignore, (actually don't know and ignore is the correct label), the invisible boy, the shadow boy, the boy beneath the stairs, was this Walter the actual subject of this fantastical soliloquy we had just heard? Confusion, no doubt, among all gathered, and *yes*, Walter as well, Ami, likely not! However, as far less than less than a few of the gathered, perhaps, only two Barry and Ami, actually knew anything at all about Walter, not even the shadow Walter, all were attentively awaiting an answer. Perhaps, this fatuous and sophistic Louise narrative actually did tell a tale! And perhaps, was this tale more than just a tale?

Walter clearly sensed a cached and cautious admiration emanating from Ami that was for certain. Ami respected Walter on the handball courts but elsewhere, Walter was painfully aware of the superior lifeblood Ami emoted with respect to all the other Walter traits, foibles and characteristics; and Walter would be the first to admit rightfully so.

But more than just Ami, a more than a few others were part of the gathering storm. As Walter observed and considered the murmurs and nodding heads moving in unison like the cilia on a giant euglena, he recognized these signals as a generalized affirmation, *yes*; an admiration from the swarm of his fictionalized behavior. A rarely experienced sanction was definitely floating in the air.

Now that question, the Ami question, an unexpected question to an unexpected turn of events, took Walter by complete surprise. When he and Louise had parted, he had thought the evening and most likely any future contact with Louise had reached its ultimate n, where n=end. He might have tried to continue or re-animate the relationship, it, this attempted breathing of life into an obviously dead relationship, had happened a few times in the past, with other terminal first dates or perhaps, it would happen in the future past, I may be mixing up Walter's past and future here, but nevertheless, in the past (or future), Walter had unsuccessfully, obviously, tried to extend terminated pre- and non-existent relationships by pleading, begging, and initiating somewhat pitiful phone calls, calls that Walter would likely have made to the hall-phone on the second floor of Louise's dorm and those calls never being answered or responded to and perhaps, the fact that those calls that were actually made and received by some classmate of hers, were never passed onto Louise (or whoever else was the intended recipient of these unwanted calls resulting from some other terminal first date). This surprising and evocative question from Ami disturbed Walter somewhat. Immediate responses needed to unanticipated questions were not in the very analytical Walter's wheelhouse. But how was he to respond to such an inquiry? It was a chess game and Walter had not even seen the board nor had he any time, whatsoever, to prepare or even think about the thousands of possible responses. Often when hit with an unexpected question, Walter, when possible, would ignore such question, but when not, he would seek a convenient neutral lie. It was in his genes; it was in the microstructures of his brain, those microstructures, as we now know, created by, both, genetic makeup and a lifetime of experiences. Those fissures and fragmentations growing and evolving as time goes on, changing with each new experience, always changing, and depending on which group of neuro-physicists and/or neurobiologists you believe, those structures have already determined what and how you are going to respond, even before you have had a chance to do so, and perhaps, before you have a choice to do so. *Again I ask do we have free will?* Walter proffers yes but only when our course of action leads to a favorable outcome. Bad decisions, unethical, nefarious, rakish and saturnalian decisions, dictating less than optimal courses of action, are obviously pre-determined by such microstructures and not within our control.

But herein, in this moment, Walter had a chance to move beyond the character he, himself, had drawn, composed, created, and identified with, as well as the character that had been drawn by his peers, classmates and contemporaries; that character being, since his matriculation at the Tute, a somewhat non-descript, easy to miss, easy to forget Walter, the Walter always studying on a Friday night and even a Saturday night, but when approached more than willing to join any group, any group whatsoever. Always happy to take a hit (we are referring here mostly to pot, hashish but who knows), to do the drug *du jour*, to help someone with their math or engineering problems, never to venture an opinion, never to complain, and always avoid confrontation. to become a good friend, a study-buddy to the girls in the dorm, but not more than that, and to pass time somewhat silently, indistinctly, abjectly, monotonously, as life continued most vibrantly, passionately, in Technicolor, in fact, for others. He was also, let's not forget, Walter the car.

Walter, however, did sense the somewhat nuanced approval in Ami's comment, "Walter, the rapist," it sounded okay, it had a tangy, provocative ring to it; buying into the fantasy, however, did have possible downsides, it didn't really happen, it didn't, no it really "Did not happen that way at all." All but two-real people, actually knew that, actually knew what was true, those being Walter and Louise. It was after all, when all factors were reduced to their most simple elements, just the fantastical emotion driven, spewing of an obviously disturbed Sagamore coed. No 'Me, too' movement in 1969 and yes, Quaaludes were involved but it was not at all in any universe fashionable or imaginable to a Bill Cosby moment. Walter had an onerous task at hand indeed, a number of alternative realities were possible, low risk, Walter-like: the anti-thesis, a higher risk and perhaps, undefined rewards in the offing, what to do?

But a quick response was needed, all this higher order thought, and narrative was being played out, instantaneously, in the moment, while Ami was standing there, in the Sagamore lounge, the half group of fifty or so eyes, at attention, waiting for a riposte to his comment, "Fuck dude, was that really you?"

For one of the few times in Walter's thus far long-lived life, including this past, which is narrative real time, and the future, which is real time present, narrative future, he played it cool, certainly not consciously evolved, just an accident and perhaps, in part due to the Hawking (mainlined but not created concept) or Feynman's (everything will happen premise) or Hugh's Sherry-infused original idea, that in the infinite number of theoretical multiverses that exist, all possible responses will ultimately occur, thus, his comment, Walter's comment, and that cool comment being, "Dude, you just don't talk about those things."[29]

It is impossible to know for sure what Walter was expecting, and the author certainly has no clue as to Walter's expectations, likely there were none, *he just did*, no thought, just action. His response was not crafted to please Ami or the group, he had no fucking idea how to do that. But as always was the case, the response would be important to Walter, he had experienced enough rejection for the night. So, for whatever time it would take, Walter waited, waiting to see what the response to his comment would be (and seriously, it was only Ami's response that would be of any importance, since the rest of the flock would follow without question). What would the outcome be to his somewhat hollow, unmeaning, purposefully amorphous but completely moment, defining and weighty comment?

---

[29] Walter assumes nor takes any credit for any decision that has been perceived as cool or as the right decision at any time leading to benefits reaped in his past or his defined and undefined future(s).

However, no immediate response from anyone was ventured, another one of those uncomfortable silences with only muffled low decibel Iron Butterfly providing provisional distraction. There was, as to be expected, a slight yet infinite (again, we invoke the Hawking, Newton, Einstein, etc., etc.,) delay, as some processing time was needed, the little hourglass icon, we all are familiar with, that nasty animation, which is fundamentally telling us to fuck-off, "You have to wait," the icon was just sitting there, there, there, some more there's, again some more there's, no change in status. The room, not the room, obviously, the room's inhabitants were processing information. These occupants, TITs, mostly consisting of future engineers and scientists, all very thoughtful and tech nerds, needed some extra time to process the heavy dialog, repartee, confab, colloquy, or exchange that was ongoing between Ami and Walter.

The hourglass disappeared and the scene, actually the complete *weltanschauung*, changed.

Ami, "Fuck you dude, well done!"

Five simple words uttered by Ami, 'Ami, the Man,' too obvious a descriptor, somewhat cheap, 'the big kahuna', even cheaper, the 'BMOC', worse by far, author's block, no Ami descriptor's other than these available, choose your own descriptor, if you must, not meaningful, of secondary importance, but the point, that point, the only point, the important point being, and that point being the meaningful five word commentary, those five words being an endorsement by Ami, a rarely experienced endorsement of Walter, and an 'implicit slap on the back', a 'Good Housekeeping Seal of Approval', a green light, hallelujah, no stopping Walter now. Walter's thrown into the wind commentary, obviously a comment he had heard at some point in his pitiful life, he obviously remembered it from somewhere, he certainly didn't think of it, likely gleaned from watching a movie, probably from a forties or fifties film noir, but this commentary led to an unexpected change in direction.

There was no longer an eerie and awkward silence permeating the XY-free freshman women's lounge on the second floor of the unnamed Sagamore College dormitory. Walter was now the hero *du jour*. Louise's tale had boded that Walter had had his way with a girl, and by all estimations in that room, fact based and thoroughly analyzed, without her taciturn approval, again, for the record completely untrue, Walter was the victim, in fact, there were no victims, and that girl was a Sagamore freshman, who was as far out of Water's league as could be imagined.

If we were in contemporary Europe (narrative future), 'Goaaaaal!' would have been proclaimed, in Chicago, Harry Caray would exclaim, "Cubs Win, Cubs win, Cubs Win,", in 1965 Boston, Johnny Most's, "Havlicek stole the ball" and even farther back in time, 1951 Russ Hodge's, "The Giants win the pennant." Perhaps, a Josh Gibson moment! A concession, some sports references to those waiting for a return to baseball, we are almost there. But this moment would and should go down, at least in younger Walter's memory banks as an event of equal import to those quoted above.

Whatever alcohol remained in the lounge was and without ceremony or conscious thought immediately consumed in its entirety, drugs as well, similar disposition, and most in attendance largely, unaware of what the drug they were so casually consuming was. But I have said this before, this was 1969 after all. Walter was already high, without any assistance, from nature's pharmacopeia, but nevertheless, he did have help; but even without such chemical fortification, the events of the evening had created a hypnogogic aura, he was in places never forth ventured; but what the fuck, he was on a roll, downsides had not appeared on the horizon, so why not consume the remaining 714s, he checked his pockets, only three left (they actually might not have all been 714s, Walter didn't bother checking), but fuck, they would do. Was this the trigger that led to Walter's six-month addiction to the god-like 'ludes'? No this was a one-off, well, maybe a two, three of four-off, that addiction, which was an addiction, would play out two years down the road, with the French Lion playing a major role. Perhaps, Walter did see the Peugeot smile! Foreshadowing, perhaps, but only in real Walter time, its narrative history! Stamps were licked, bongs were lit, and a general pandemonium ensued. A celebration of nerds!

The home-fires had done their job, Homer had returned to Troy, there's obviously some higher order geographical pun here, but let's skip that for now. Walter was Homer, an epic hero, at least for a short few moments.

The celebration continued, it lasted a few frantic hours, perhaps more, no more need to discuss time compressibility, you have all gotten the idea by now; the embers were dying, only ashes remained, only metaphorically. The end point of this Saturday night celebration was determined only when all drugs and food were consumed. But it was Ami, as it was and is always Ami, who put an end to the evening, he who proclaimed it was time to move on. Ami, the forever composed Ami, even when completely wasted, and Ami sensing the Tute confederacy of nerds might attract unwanted attention from local authorities, decided now was the time to 'Leave Dodge.' Adding to that was the simple fact he was immersed in a room full of males, only males, and he had no possible chance of getting laid. Well, that might not be quite true, as the Younger recalls, since Ami did make a casual, an understated move, and he repeated that understated 'move' several times, and that move being a more than casual squeeze to and rub of Walter's shoulder's, so perhaps there…but no never mind that, let's leave that for another time. It was now time to move on.

Another scene change, impending not quite there yet, the party ended, important discussions and negotiations regarding transportation back to the Tute commenced. The magical Peugeot was overloaded, Walter, Ami, Barry, several other walk-ons, seven in a car designed for five at most.

We, now, move on, and jump ahead to the real Sunday morning, back at the 'Tute', although it was technically Sunday morning in the previous scene, the Sagamore lounge, but, *no*, those nether hours of Sunday morning, the times for not sleeping but partying, those are not really Sunday morning. The Sunday morning we are now referring to is simply the time to 'get the fuck up.'

Sunday morning, and *yes*, it might have been the afternoon, but whatever time it was, it was the time Walter returned to the living, coming back to consciousness, slowly, it took quite a while, disequilibrium, dry mouth, pounding in the ears, headache; temple area, maybe back of the neck, especially if in your younger days (narrative future), you happened to be thrown or will be thrown through the windshield of a foreign car, I'm sure most readers are familiar with such, if not, give it a try (you really should try it at least once, the pleasure of such pain and if confused what I'm suggesting doing is doing whatever caused the hangover, drugs, alcohol, hopefully, both, not flying through the windshield of a Peugeot).

Walter was slowly returning to the land of the living in the lobby of some dorm-like structure, at this point in time, unbeknownst to him, he was still one with the carpet but was making progress. His face was no longer loosely bonded to the puddle of drool, which Walter only hoped was his; an elbow then two, after some more effort, he made it to the referee's wrestling position, then, with considerable effort, he was upright. He mind was clearing a bit, he could feel his IQ increasing exponentially; from this now elevated view, he noticed he was surrounded (more like standing among fallen soldiers) by Barry and a number of other known and unrecognized TIT hall residents and perhaps, other freshman from foreign dorms or perhaps, even Troilet students, all still tightly bound to the lowest horizontal level of this dorm-like structure.

Walter slowly looked about and surveyed his surroundings, it only took a few moments more to realize where he was; it was the lobby of the Nathan Hall Dorm. At first, he had thought he might still be at Sagamore. More brain cells came online, likely now close to full operating speed; without any emotion, concern, thought, empathy, and with perhaps a conscious avowal, he simply and methodically stepped over the prone bodies, the collected mass of human destruction, and ambled over to the dorm lobby entrance, glanced outside and ingurgitated the brightness, the innocence, and the radiance of this new day; however, quickly his focus shifted, and he shielding his eyes, as they were quite sensitive to this morning newness, honed (maybe, homed) in on the parking lot adjacent to the dorm.

The day was sunny, blindingly clear, not a hint of fog or clouds, the morning we all hope for but see perhaps fewer than a handful of days each year. The perfect morning to greet you, to shake your mind free from that massive, alcohol, drug, and experiential induced hangover. Walter opened the dormitory's double doors facing the parking lot and he was assaulted by an effluence of air that smelled fresh, clean, and undisturbed; it might have been morning, perhaps afternoon, but it was a Sunday morning, at a college, where Saturday night partying was the norm, so it was disturbingly but not unsurprisingly quiet. The sun was hidden by one of the taller dorm buildings so its position, where it sat in the sky, couldn't help Walter approximate the time of day.

Without effort, just a slight turn of the head, Walter noticed that there, no more than thirty paces from that entrance, and sitting off to the right, was the magical Peugeot 404. The Peugeot, reflecting the blazing sun like a not too clean mirror, was ominously silent. The lot was pretty empty and the Peugeot was parked at an angle, it was parked on the diagonal and thus, was taking up two spaces. No other cars were nearby, perhaps, they sensed the Peugeot needed alone time. The Peugeot occupied its space and time quietly, if not precisely; it existed lifelessly, it was after all simply composed of just metal, glass, and plastic, it was not animated, it was not real, it had no life, other than what we chose to give it. We, collectively, as a species, anthropomorphize our vehicles, give them names and personalities, we love them and want them to be real, but after all, aren't they all just conveniences and conveyances, simply means of getting us from point A to B. Logically, we know this animation is folly, and recognize the silliness of it, but inside each of us, on a deeper level, don't we know that what is really true is not necessarily true. Do we know what we think we know; we all believe in things that we really shouldn't believe in? Is it all that simple? There are no algorithms, there are no real answers, looking at the big picture, are we simply not ants trying to play chess? Check, I think, as in checkmate, not check please! But is it any more absurd to personify a vehicle that we are so dependent upon, as it is to believe in a supreme deity, god, creator, holiness, Jehovah, Yahweh, Jah, or Allah, each of these coming to life, thousands of years in the distant past, and each based upon myth or a simple narrative that has been lucky enough to survive the test of time. How many possible Gods, religions, and miracles have been lost, simply not told because some continuing cultural tale or papyrus transcribed by monks, was, until it was not, until it was lost forever? Why are these beliefs more important more real than possible sentience in chunk of metal? Answer, please! Where is the proof? Not proffered thus far! Faith! I have faith in what I can see and touch. And then…

Speculation aside, back to perceived reality, what did happen, was the completely lifeless and metal forged Peugeot, at the precise instant Walter recognized its essence in the Nathan Hall parking lot, chose to reveal its sentience and its true nature and present a knowing smile to Walter. That knowing smile on its face being comprised of the grill, the two circular headlights housing, both high and low beams, and centered within the grill, and most importantly, the Peugeot logo, a lion's head with flowing mane. Walter thought he saw the Lion wink at him but this was clearly a leftover mild hallucination, the result of an excess of drugs, alcohol, and the unexpected and rarely to be encountered, past and future, sexual stimulation. Walter blinked, squinted, and refocused; he rubbed his fists into his eyes like a baby awakening, but even, after all, this, he still saw the Lion looking back at him with that knowing smile. Walter shook his head, closed his eyes and tried to fixate, visualize, and retrace his steps and the events of the evening past. Snippets of conversation, scenes, one by one, returning to his consciousness, the previous evening's tapestry was somewhat complete, but not quite so. In spite of such orchestrations, when he, again, turned his attention back to the Peugeot, a smile was still evident upon the magical vehicle.

Walter quickly reviewed, and with feelings that might be defined as panic, certainly anxiety, he hastily reconstructed his cerebral video of the eve past. However, there were substantial portions of that evening missing, somehow erased or perhaps never recorded, and of these memories, the most important being, each and all events subsequent to the 'after-rape party' and concerning the return trip to the TIT.

Walter was unable to focus, as the disturbingly real, unreal, hallucinatory French Lion smile was drawing him away from his task at hand, that task being finding out 'what the fuck happened after leaving the Sagamore common area.'

This Saturday Night Puzzle needed to be solved and Walter was up for the task. And the answer to that puzzle, the seemingly only missing piece of information about last night's safari, was staring him just thirty yards in the distance. That previous evening in Saratoga, after exiting the Sagamore dorm, Walter had trekked, with what we might go as far as to venture, was with, at this point in time, his newly created 'crew.' Completely looped, they were, stoned, wasted, baked, stewed, smashed, ripped, fried, and strung out, not an ounce of sobriety among the group (and by the way, what is an ounce of sobriety, can it be weighed); and this hapless ensemble ventured forth from the dorm, somehow managing to find the Peugeot, and then all seven, seven, at least, seven of them, all completely drunk, stoned, high from some intoxicant, not a one sober or in control of any of their wits or perhaps, biological functions, Walter and the six plus, including Ami, all piled into the car, Walter (perhaps) into the driver's seat.

Next stop—TIT dorm, Nathan Hall, sometime Sunday after sunrise and before dusk

Walter hadn't given a thought as how the return trip back to the TIT unfolded, at least, not until he regained some clarity and consciousness on this quite clear and wondrous Sunday morning. In fact, why would he have, the blissed catatonic state he chose to put himself him (and this happened quite often) was definitely a survival mechanism. But now, upon awakening and staring, seemingly mesmerized by the Lion's crafty smile, Walter took that smile as a challenge and the Lion was simply asking, "Walter are you missing something?" And just seconds after realizing there was a question, Walter understood what the question was and that question being how did that magical Lion get from point A, Sagamore College, early Sunday morning, to point B, the TIT, sometime later Sunday morn?

Walter knows, or thinks he knows, that he began his thirty-mile journey behind the wheel, in the driver's seat, caressed by the soft imitation, leather burgundy vinyl, in complete control of that French 'Panthera Leo.' Sometime later, he, and as best as he can recall, ended up in the dorm lobby, making love to the shabby indoor-outdoor green-grey carpeting, along with the plus six (in fact, quite a few more than six, since when the other dorms had heard of the Nathan Hall adventures at Sagamore, quite a few more freshman headed over to Nathan Hall and an after-party, after-party went on for who knows how long. No details remain from this historically distant celebration.) However, after a hasty assessment of the people inventory, notably missing from the scattered human waste was Ami.

Walter mindlessly and with some effort cast aside, the double doors of the Nathan Hall main entrance. He was still a bit subpar, and with some difficulty, he walked, perhaps staggered is more appropriate, his reduced performance the result of the lasting effects from the drugs, alcohol, poisons, intoxicants, whatever, from the previous twelve or so hours, and as best he could manage, he continued walking towards the awaiting car. The Peugeot was unlocked and surprisingly, the keys were in the ignition. He thoughtlessly pocketed the keys and prepared to collapse into the driver's seat, regain familiarly with the smiling beast, his companion, and to be so for at least two more years, and perhaps recover his dignity and sanity, wrapped in the luxury of the imitation leather, French vinyl. But alas, *no*, not possible, the seat was situated into such a forward position that it was impossible for Walter to squeeze into the gap between the seat and the steering wheel. The 1966 Peugeot 404 had an adjustable steering wheel, an advanced feature for such times, and this was positioned so low that it further impeded Walter's attempts to enter into that the confined space.

Walter was not big, perhaps 150 pounds and five foot, eight inches at the time, but based on the physical limitations and ergo-dynamic principals, a term not in common use in 1969, he clearly did not drive the car from Saratoga to Troy, NY. Well, maybe, he did, and we might ascribe the position of the seat and the steering wheel to the highly unlikely scenario wherein, after driving some thirty miles or so in a completely unconscious state, he, Walter, for some reason, after arriving at the dorms, exited the vehicle and manually adjusted the seat to its most forward position and lowered the position of the steering wheel to its lowest position. A possibility for sure, but Occam's razor states an emphatic no! Group consensus, Walter did not drive the magical Peugeot from the Sagamore parking lot, returning the some thirty miles to the parking lot adjacent to

Nathan Hall, and let's add to that in a completely unconscious and intoxicated state.

It is exceedingly likely, in fact, a very high confidence level, that a quite small person, no more than five feet zero, was the navigator and guide leading the seven unconscious samurai safely back to the TIT. Regrettably, historical records and anecdotes suggest that St. Christopher (the Saint ensuring travelers safety) was quite tall, perhaps, even a giant for the times, so that doesn't seem to be a possibility. Also, as Walter remembers, and it is only a vague memory, that he was the smallest of the group of TIT warriors that returned from their conquest of Sagamore. Regrettably, no real, meaningful, or even fanciful answers forthcoming then, now, and unlikely in the future.

A true mystery unsolved to this day. Throughout the unpredictable journey, each of our lives takes one often experiences unsolvable mysteries such as these. And to be sure, many of these unsolved mysteries occur in proximity to events involving excess alcohol consumption or drug use and perhaps, head trauma as well. It's quite easy and convenient to surmise such mysterious are simply due to lack of processed information resulting from diminished capacity, but may I inject a thought that perhaps such mysteries only show themselves when we are unfettered by the constraints of everyday logic, clarity of mind, and reasoning. Thus, is it possible that in such a garbled state, perhaps, we can accept the unacceptable? Just a speculation, thrown out onto the winds, likely complete garbage, and completely unrelated to this narrative, so let's move on. But as you hopefully recall, earlier in this narrative, Walter's somewhat thrown out comment in response to an Ami question, and in real perspective, likely equal to the dismal prattle herein expounded upon, did result in quite a fascinating outcome, so…

For the next several months, Walter enjoyed a demi-celebrity status as the main character in the Saturday Night Café Lena Narrative. A few 'kudos' to Walter were acknowledged, some high fives, the first, the second, and perhaps the third hits on the water pipe, something of a tribute, but no, in fact, in these times, actually more of a real value that you might imagine now, but nothing of tangible substance, no real or lasting rewards. And as all things do or seem to do, the events of that early October evening with the magical Peugeot, with Barry, with Ami, with Louise, and with the supporting cast of characters, that evening, without thought or celebration, receded into nothingness, as if it being a droplet of water, its size diminishing as it evaporates in the sun of the day. By Christmas break, Walter had returned to the land of the dead. He was once again only Walter, the nerd in room 210, the rapist moniker was only a past life. While others lived in the moment, grabbed what was offered, and followed the sage advice, that advice embraced by an entire generation, and it being badly misquoted as, loving whomever you happened to be with at the moment, Walter regressed, and returned to the default state, became somewhat embryonic, germinal, and inchoate. He observed, he viewed, he analyzed, but he dared not get too close to the flickering flame of life, *oh* the incalculable downsides therein! After all, we all remember Icarus!

********

Sports fans rejoice; we have ended this painful digression and return to the world of Little League baseball, in fact, the actual conclusion to this tale.

However, again, I have lied, before we return to the joys of the great American pastime (and I am referring to baseball and not sex) two points to ponder:

The first point—to this day and this day being almost fifty years hence from the Café Lena milestone, the person or the spirit, the sprite, the fay, the fairy, the nymph, or the dryad, perhaps, unlikely as it is, the TIT or Sagamore student, who drove the Magical 404 from Sagamore, in Saratoga, NY to the TIT in Troy, NY, some thirty miles south, is unknown and is still a complete (and I do mean complete, no clues or possible candidates, after all, it is almost fifty years from this meaningless but significant incident) mystery. It will likely remain such, long after the existence of all the participants orchestrating that magical Saturday night ceases to be.

Also it is absolutely true, and as stated before or perhaps soon to be stated, Walter adamantly denies the existence of any form of deity or supreme or guiding being (and he strongly believes that anyone with at least half a brain and not prone to episodes of delusion, should be of similar orchestration). Accordingly the intervention of such a hallucination (aka deity) could in no way account for, in any way whatsoever, any reshaping of the events leading to the safe culmination of that memorable evening. However, as all participants, in the aforementioned journey were in a state of complete 'waste-hood', the fact those participants did arrive home safely does, in fact, bode, if you have any open mindedness whatsoever, that there is/was or might have been/be an indemonstrable force intervening in the proceedings of that evening. Simply a thought, exceedingly unlikely, definitely non-Walter, but as both Walter and the author age, some aspects of open mindedness occasionally visit and contemplating the 'uncontemplatable', sometimes, against our most profound wishes, just happens!

The second point—

********

I seem to have forgotten the second point, the plausible explosiveness of the conclusion to the first point leaves me completely thoughtless.

Scene change—back to baseball! Finally.

# Part 6
## The First Swing

The Roundabout Club of New Apley was a well-respected organization, a gathering of local businessmen, who, for the most part, were far more successful than Walter's dad. As a rule, most of the members were community leaders, not necessarily the top tier, not those running 'the show', but the general membership likely included men just beneath this loftiest echelon, those men who had enough time and interest to be involved in such organizations and to oversee the somewhat tedious administrations of a small town. These were the sergeants of an organization, not leading but effecting, men of action, men familiar with getting things done, these were the men who executed the sundry operations of small towns. Their forte were matters of insignificance! Unquestionably, these Roundabout meetings were in a sense, high school reunions, a gathering of former team captains, alpha-males, athletically gifted or not, bullies, successful legacy business owners (most with insufficient brain power to continue a legacy, therefore, it was granted they would undeniably run their endowed businesses into nothingness, a throwback reference to the 'regression to the mean' concept) and their respective entourages. Not in anyone's wildest dreams would these groups have included valedictorians or salutatorians, as in all probability, those intellectually superior specimens, yet of diminished high school value, had migrated on to communities offering more opportunity and potential. In fact, one of the many community functions of this and similar organizations was to sponsor a Little League Team. Sports continued to play (and, in fact, does to this day as well) an important role in the lives of these former high school celebrities, only now, rather than playing themselves, they have deferred to their offspring, hoping the glory road would live on or perhaps, new heights were yet to be achieved. Still in existence today, the Roundabout Club of New Apley, a member of the Roundabout International Order, since 1911, had and still has the following mission statement, this statement vaguely recalled and summarized from their published mission statement posted on some fictional web site.

'The Roundabout Club of New Apley, MA is a community service-based organization comprised of professionals and community members committed to enhancing the lives of the residents of the communities of New Apley, Clarksland and Apley.'

This statement is as true today as it was in the 1960s, long before the idea of an International Order of Roundarians website existed. It is still true today, despite a massive global change in values, no a deterioration of values to be more accurate (I think we can be quantitative here and not reject the idea that values are not simply a subjective concept, I side with George Apley on this point and he was espousing such a radical position from an early twentieth century fictional perspective). We have all witnessed and perhaps, passively accepted or ignored or in a defensive only strategy, simply tried to keep the stilt grass out of own little acre, a dissolution of the importance of family, inherent morality, self-worth, purpose, and an appreciation of the value of achievement. And perhaps, most importantly, the actual derision of the value of a solid day of work, regardless of the intrinsic value of that day of work (hard to really determine such an undeterminable value), I can go on, but will stop here, except for this last point and although I have no reason to posit this, and I'm sure, I have no proof, nevertheless, I surely and truly believe, this erosion of values has been less dramatic in communities such as New Apley and other sister communities. But this is simply speculation, today, the older Walter (and the author as well) are so far from New Apley, physically, only one hundred miles or so, but an infinite number of mind[30] zones that neither could possibly know for sure. Of course, the influence of organizations,

---

[30] A mind-zone is the younger Walter's short-hand expression and completely arbitrary term, somewhat linked to an individual's evolution of values over real time, space, and experience. To visualize, consider a three-dimensional free space, with, perhaps, the x-axis representing real time, the y-axis physical distance and the z-axis personal growth (experience). And each axis is not linear or in any sense equal to the others, as change in one dimension may be far more important in determining the ultimate distance from A to B than others. It's pretty clear that the z-axis, and that being experience, far outweighs, the importance of the other axes, in this particular case, those being about forty years passage of time or so and a distance of a mere one hundred miles.

such as the Roundabout Society, were far greater in these small, dispiriting, lifeless, bromidic, dreary, glum, pedestrian, colorless, forlorn, depressive, unvaried, plodding, and banausic towns such as the 1960s New Apley compared to, for example, larger towns and cities, those towns and cities having a greater variety of activities, including academic, social, artistic, recreational, and cultural. But no, let's not rewrite, for we cannot rewrite history, New Apley was what it was, and the Roundabouts and similar groups were of significant local import. You cannot lead the life you did not lead!

But why so much about the Roundabout Club of New Apley, why not the VFW (Veterans of Foreign War's), the Elks (BPOE), or other equally important social groups? Simply put, Walter played on the Roundabout sponsored Little League team, the team, if you were asked what team you were on, you likely replied "The Roundarians,", one of the six teams in the New Apley Little League in 1960.

As a junior or perhaps a senior in high school, Walter cannot be quite certain of which year it was, if he had to bet, he would volunteer senior year as most awards were, in fact, given out senior year, he was chosen to receive the Jr. Roundabout Scholar Award; this award was given to an outstanding student who exhibited the values of the Roundabout Society of New Apley (those expatiated upon earlier). Why he received this award was a puzzle to Walter, but not to the Stafford family collective, whom, as we have already made reference to, firmly believed that the younger Walter was deserving and should receive any and every possible award that was to be given, regardless as to the selection criteria for such awards (the older Walter does now agree with their position). Perhaps, his selection was in part or completely due to the fact he was on the Roundabout Little League team, although that event was at least five years in the rearview mirror. Such casual relationships are easily and quickly lost in small town *Americana*, furthermore, his performance for that team was not exceptional, other than his role in the short tale, the main substance, and conclusion of we are now rapidly approaching.

Walter was undoubtedly, by far, and by a lot, and not by just a little, a lot, really a lot, did I say by a lot, the best, the preeminent, the primo, the nonpareil, the peerless, and unparalleled student academically (and BTW, these are younger Walter's words, so you can be the judge of their factuality), at Drumly Regional High School (often referred to by some of the five hundred or so students as Dreary Reg). This superiority was decidedly true in all things math and science and in fact, any class not directly related to verbal skills, no contest whatsoever. Walter did well enough in those other subjects, such as language(s) or history, those which he considered peripheral subjects, and well enough means A2 or A1, both designations somewhat vague and arbitrary but often these courses did require some effort something Walter found and this was true throughout all his schooling, his academic, and his professional career as well, that he rarely needed to do, second or third gear was often good enough to be 99+ percentile. But academics notwithstanding, Walter in no way exhibited any of the community, leadership, or societal values the Roundabout Society embraced. Walter was and continues to this day, to some degree, to be an observer, a non-participant, the

Walter shadow. In fact, it wasn't until the middle of senior year, just after the first of the year, where upon the high school principal of dreary Drumly Regional High School, a stuffy and somewhat pompous, sententious, and officious character, perfect for the job, in fact, whom the students did and we will here also refer to as Principal Chrome Dome, that sobriquet existed for obvious reasons, summoned Walter to his office for a Walter meet and greet as the Principal was astounded, amazed, befuddled, baffled, perplexed, dismayed, and annoyed that the leading candidate (by a lot) for the honors of being the graduating class valedictorian was someone unknown to old CD and his inner-circle. The meeting was short.

"So, you are the mysterious Walter, whom I've just learned ranks number one in academic status for the senior class. You seem to have a 101.8 grade point average, and as far as I can recall, I have never met you, talked to you, or had any contact at all. In fact, you don't look the least bit familiar to me and your transcript does indicate you have been here for almost four full years. Doesn't that surprise you, as it certainly surprises the bejeezus out of me?" [31]

---

[31] Your numerical grade value was determined by your actual class average based upon tests and whatnot and then points were added to that number, usually one point for college prep courses, two or three points for honors courses, perhaps, five or so for AP courses, and even more points if you were allowed to take a course at the local college back then called New Apley State College. Walter was at a decided disadvantage in the race for valedictorian, since not until his junior year, was Walter placed into a single honors course, never-mind an AP course.

No response from Walter, probably nervous, or simply not interested. More likely, Walter was scared shitless, a default state, but a state, which then and throughout the years, Walter seemed to convince others (and this 'convincement' was not directed just accidental and the others usually being the parties bringing on a potential conflictual encounter) that this shitless freight was a feigned state and any freight that did exist, did not exist at all, and this perhaps, confusing the potential confronting party and leading such party to think or speculate that their nuanced interpretation of his (Walter's) insecurity, was possibly in error and this Walter reaction was just a well-developed laid back 'tude' and perhaps, this Dude (with the 'tude') should not be underestimated. So, the opposition, aka confronting party, would adopt the conservative position and reckon, "Let's be cautious here, let's not conflate insecurity with relaxed self-assurance,", for that could be a social disaster as "There might be more than we see at the surface."

(By the way, totally not true, Walter was scared shitless most of the time, then and now, and I should know!)

Principal Chrome Dome, "Now, Walter can I be assured that you are going to get a haircut for graduation, it's quite long, almost looks like you might have been cutting it yourself."

*No way am I getting a haircut and who cares who's cutting it.*

That response, only a passing thought, Walter's real retort a simple, "Sure,", reflective, no thinking or analysis involved, no added or superlative narrative, why waste words; Walter, knowing this response, would mollify the principal, and end the conversation, or at least, he hoped it would end it and that was the point. And, of course, Walter didn't have the slightest intention of getting a haircut, or to be more exact, cutting his own hair; something he still does on occasions to this very day. Walter and the principal had this discussion in the early spring of 1969 and his hair was not really long for the time. After all, 1969 has oft been described as 'The year of Love', this was the Woodstock[32] generation, a true inflection point in time, altering, forever, the norms and behavior from times past. Peace, love, Crosby Stills, and Nash etc., etc. Walter's hair was mid-ear length and could be described as a pageboy, a Beatles, or a Moe from the Three Stooges, cut.

Principal Dome, "There is still a possibility you won't be the valedictorian, you only have a 1.9 grade point average lead, even factoring in credits for advanced courses, which surprisingly you seem to lack, and I notice you are taking all honors courses this semester. I am a bit concerned this is something you haven't done in the past. Perhaps, you are overextending yourself."

---

[32] While Woodstock was being held, Walter declined an invite from several friends who were attending. He, along with the family, the four of them, journeyed off to southern ME, for what was to be the last glorious family vacation, a celebration of life, as it was for the four of them. An end, the last annualization of a non-tradition. Walter's friends, after they recovered their sobriety a week or so after the event, reported back to Walter, descriptions of a transcendental life altering experience. When Walter thinks back to that time and considers the decision he made, he always comes to the conclusion the only choice was southern ME. Free will, phooey!

This was a pointed warning and perhaps a little 'mind gamesmanship' from the Principal and likely, a hope that immersion in these so called honors courses would overwhelm Walter, he would not be able to stand the pressure, would fall apart, his grades would drop, and one of the chosen, those students who were placed in honors classes from grade six and onward, those students being the sons and daughters of the community doctors, lawyers, successful business owners, and in one case, the daughter of a Williams College professor, would flourish, prevail and supplant Walter, Walter with the too long hair, as the 1969 Valedictorian at Dreary Regional High School.

Walter's response was terse, "Oh, Okay,", not really an appropriate of meaningful reply, today, the response would obviously be "Whatever,", but not really in use in the 1960s.[33]

So, while he clearly had the academic credentials, Walter did not embody the Roundarian ethos; he was pretty much invisible throughout high school, he had no shadow or perhaps, he was a shadow. While life was flashing past him, moving forward on the screen of Cullen's Drive-In Movie Theater, Walter would occasionally look up at that those scenes, observe happy people enjoying life, engaging, feeling, being, he, himself, wanting to be to in those scenes,

---

[33] BTW, Walter did end up being the valedictorian, *numero uno*, in the class of 1969 of some two hundred plus students. For his graduation address, Walter started out, high probability a start quite similar to at least 25% of all such addresses, "Today, as we move beyond our years at…" Regrettably or perhaps, thankfully, that is all that remains of that quite likely lackluster speech.

but more likely, scurrying back and forth to the snack bar, from car to snack bar, pick up a hot dog, loaded with so much condiment you could barely make out the dog, and fries, here again camouflaged with ketchup, and then scurry back to the car. Within the safety of the car, he within the womb of the Stafford family, life could be observed, no participation was required, no feelings necessary, complete control, no surprises.

Looking back, Walter firmly believes this Roundabout award was a bone toss, there was a conscious decision made by someone or a group of some ones, somewhere. The three or four other male academic stars had each won numerous awards, had been elected president of this and that, honored here and there; there had not been to date any award given to Walter, the student most excellent. He had won a few academic contests, but these were so specialized and trivial they didn't make it into the mainstream. Since Walter was a former member of the Roundabout Little League team, Walter believes that a decision was made that Walter, albeit an outlier, and not truly fitting the Roundarian's values, was indeed the top student and needed an award, so let's give him this one, the Jr. Roundarian Scholar.

End scene.

So, let's go back to the title of this narrative and finally explain why the title (it's actually the subtitle we are concerned with, the title '*The Walter Integral*' has been fully explained upfront, in fact, before the author's forward) is referencing Depend™ Adult Undergarments and paying respect to DFW. So, why Depend™? Clearly, you already grasp this point, it's pretty obvious by now, I tried to, somewhat obliquely make it clear without actually saying anything. Undeniably, you now know quite a bit about the younger Walter, perhaps, more than you would care to. Nevertheless, to bring to an end…without further delay, dawdling obfuscation, fogging an already fogged issue, the connection to Depends™ is, Walter was so nervous, for the many reasons stated above and more to be expiated upon later (or perhaps, already told), there was the highest probability that each time he got up to bat for most of his full first year, his nine-year-old year in Little League, *he peed his pants*. Not just a little trickle, not merely a few drops, but a full and complete release, involving, both, the autonomic and somatic nervous system, zero control, perhaps, four to eight ounces of yellow, slightly acidic urine flowing into the wool Roundabout uniform, obviously at a prominent location where you would expect it to flow, (his loins, his groin, the wiener area, little Walter's home, etc.), usually just before or after the first pitch of each and every at bat. Conceivably up until right now and prior to this disclosure (and the author might be completely delusional in espousing this view) the only living person who knows of this fact is, in fact, Walter. It is conceivable his older sister knew and knows, but we will leave that alone for now.

Walter never experienced this problem throughout the pre-season, which mostly consisted of drills, batting and fielding practice, no pressure, nothing of importance, no practice games, but as he came up to bat for the first time in the first game of that first season, little Walter knew exactly what was about to happen and he knew that with a certainty that he rarely, if ever, experienced.

The God's did speak that day!

As Walter was about to enter the batter's box, the Gods (whatever that means and it's a very personal definition for sure), these Gods, whom the younger Walter most assertively did not (and arguably does not) believe in, (and for the record, countless others espouse a similar view, the Younger was not unique in his belief, possibly unique within his immediate family of six) but these Gods, who clearly must have existed at least for a moment, they made themselves apparent, only by action, conspiring with the weather, or perhaps the weather God (or is it the God of Weather), regardless, and 'they, whoever' decided it should rain, and rain at the exact moment it should, that exact moment being as younger Walter entered the batter's box and was about to 'unload.' And this godly apparition provided rain, just enough rain to drench the uniforms of all the players, including younger Walter, and enough rain to mask the ever-widening darkened wet spot growing from the Younger's loin area, but not enough rain, to make the field unplayable and necessitating a calling off of the game. Thus Walter's outpouring of emotion and his very physical outpouring of urine was outpoured by the rain itself and the more than dribble of the aforementioned urine diffusing through his uniform, Roundabout grey with a burgundy number nine on the back, went unnoticed, masked by the more than modest sprinkle, thus, a disaster averted or at least, delayed. (BTW, Roundabout lost that game 11-7, Walter walked three times (peed three times as well), scored twice and stuck out once (peed a fourth time), never once lifting his bat off his less than mighty shoulder.)

Walter's more than just a tinkle micturition went unnoticed, for at least several days after the game, hiding in time until Walter's mother, back at the Stafford family's home, gathering up his uniform for cleaning, although a wool uniform, it was washed and not dry-cleaned, and upon collecting the uniform, along with a sundry of other items of clothing from both Walter and his sister, she noticed, and it was impossible to miss, and she did not miss, the decidedly nitrogenous, litterbox-like 'urinish' smell, with a few days of ad hoc fermentation enriching the odor, emanating from the pile of collected dirties, and upon mom's further investigation, traced this perfume of body function to Walter's number nine Roundabout uniform.

"Butchie, come down here," instructed Walter's perplexed mom. Butchie or Butch was Walter's nickname, named after his haircut, a butch, slicked back with pomade, a haircut, which Walter sported for many years, the actual timeframe undeterminable at this time but certainly throughout his Little League years. (We may have introduced Butchie earlier without such elaboration).

Younger Walter or henceforth, but only sometimes and arbitrarily so, we will refer to as Butch or Butchie, Butch replied, "I'm busy mom, what do ya want?"

"I need to see you now; you know what that means and I AM NOT GOING TO ASK YOU AGAIN."

Butch accommodated his mom's request for an audience as he always did, maybe it was a demand actually, only nuanced differences far beyond young Butchie's ability to discern. He might not have been a good son (one never really knows, you can't get inside the head of a parent) but at least, he was an obedient one. Thoughtlessly and unknowing of what was about to transpire, he began his short trip, cautiously navigating the narrow and somewhat decrepit stairwell, fourteen steps (counted hundreds of times) leading from the three, small, upstairs bedrooms, to a short, no more than twelve feet long hallway, at the bottom of the stairs, this hallway leading to the sleeping porch, if you took a left at the bottom (rarely taken, as it was the den of his grandmother, Vera), or towards mom and the kitchen, if you took a right-hand turn. Very worn, threadbare, non-descript carpeting, fraying at the edges, not attached well at all, an accident, which never happened, waiting to happen, lots of shed dog's hairs actually keeping the woolen carpet from disintegrating, completely covered the treads. The stairs exhibiting a slight dogleg to the right, somewhere, in the middle. At the bottom, Walter took the right, and met his mother in the smallish kitchen, the focal point of the household and the main gathering point for the extended Stafford family, which included the two Walter's, Walter's wife or mom, Walter's sister or daughter, designation, depending on which of the Walter perspectives you choose. Henceforth, to save time unless specifically stated or obvious, the younger Walter will be the perspective of choice. Also, included in the family were Mrs. Stafford's brother, Al, we met Al already, and their mom Vera (the Younger Walter's nonna referred to by all as 'Little Nonni', which is a bit of a redundancy, since in Italian, *nonnina* often shortened to *nonni* means little grandmother), who, at this point in time, was confined to a wheel chair or on occasion, using a walker with great difficulty, the result of an accident several years pre-dating the 'Great Pee', being knocked over, while shopping in the local A and P[34], by an unsupervised child. Somewhat unexpected back then (I'm referring to unsupervised children) generally speaking children were on a much shorter tether, but certainly common-place, now, with the all too common distracted mothering, multi-tasking, texting, the promiscuous use of nannies, lack of discipline, manners, common decency, going to stop here, lots more possible.

"Butchie, want to tell me about your uniform."
Mom was being intentionally cryptic, a good strategy, she wanted Butchie to make the first move.

"Yeah, it's kinda dirty, guess it was the rain, you remember it rained pretty hard that day, lots of mud. But I did score three runs member?"

"Yes I remember but I think there is more here than rain and runs to talk about."

"Mom, I'm not sure I know what you are talking about."

"Well, you didn't poop your pants but there is no doubt that you peed them," responded Mrs. Stafford, the decibel level ascending with each word, and she nervously smoking her hand rolled cigarette, it spending more time in her hand than her mouth and she paying far more attention to the

---

[34] Herein, we are referring to the Great Atlantic and Pacific Tea Company national chain of grocery stores, not the John Updike short story of the same name but certainly, worth a read. In short, A and P was founded in the late 19th century and for about sixty years, was the largest company in America, based on revenue. The Wall Street Journal called it the Walmart before Walmart. After years of mismanagement and failure to modernize, the final version of the company, after several unsuccessful Chapter 11 filings, closed its doors for good in 2016.

cigarette than little Butchie, this not being a conversation Mrs. Stafford wanted to engage in.

The tone of his mother's voice puzzled and somewhat alarmed Butchie (more than the words, in fact), as he was not accustomed to any reprimand whatsoever, or even of the raising of a parental voice, as he being, the albeit, somewhat obese child, he was also the precious, priceless, and precocious child who could do no wrong.

Butch, "Mom, seriously I'm not a baby," pleadingly, *I really do not want to start this conversation; got an idea where it's going*!

Mom, "What else can I say Butchie, it smells a lot like pee to me, go ahead give it a smell."

"Yuk, I'm not going to smell it, come on Mom it wasn't me, really."

"What do you mean it was wasn't you, are you saying someone peed on you at the game?"

"Yeah, right, that's it, good sleuthing mom, I didn't want to tell you, it didn't smell that bad when I got home, I figured you would miss it, my other clothes smelling pretty bad on their own. It must have umh…"

*Better think this out*

Right then and there, and as he experienced the journey to adulthood and past, Walter, aka little Butchie, was easily seduced by the convenient, the uncomplicated, the opportune painless lie, the path of least resistance. However, Butchie immediately realized pursuing the getting peed on story by someone else had too many downsides, quickly his mind flipped through the endless possibilities, sorting out alternative scenes, as if they were chess moves. After a rapid, yet thorough analysis, he realized, however, that each, even the most remotely possible getting peed on scenarios, ended up in a worse checkmate than the current situation. Dead-end decision tree here.

Another thrust tried, "No that's not it, it must have been Duke, Mom. It wasn't me that's for sure."

*Yeah, that's gonna work, Duke gets the blame.*

"Really, Butchie, he never pees in the house and besides, you know he's too old to climb the stairs anyway."

*Parried well mom!*

"Honestly, Mom, I don't know how the pee, if it really is pee, got there."

"Well, I'm not sure what happened either. I think we are at a standoff here, unless there's more to add?"

"Nope, no more to add, that's it!"

*That was close*

"Well, I guess the only question left is do you think it's going to happen again?"

*Didn't see that coming*

"Mother, upon further reflection," Walter certainly could be a pompous little asshole, especially for someone caught peeing their baseball uniform, "I think it was the rain, it might have been the four cokes I drank before the game; I don't think the hot dogs or the chips had anything to do with it. I'm sure it was the rain. It triggered something. It might rain again; maybe, I should play only when it rains."

*Nailed it!*

"Well if the rain triggered it..."

"And, Mom, we still aren't sure what it is

"As I was saying, if the rain triggered the episode!" (BTW highly unlikely Mrs. Smith would have used this word, likely a Butchie revision over the years) then you should play only when it doesn't rain."

"Sure, that makes…but no, no, that's not gonna work because… Mom honestly, you really can't be sure that its pee on the uniform. You know I throw my underwear into the dirty clothes pile right on top of the uniform and you only do laundry once a week"

Butchie saw his mon was not too pleased with these comments so he moved on.

Sometimes, I don't jiggle after peeing, so it's possible that a few drops, here and there, from all my underwear leaked onto the uniform, and actually, now, that I've thought this through, I am pretty sure that's what you smell, the jiggle pee."

*Finally I think we are finished here*

"That's a whole lot of pee smell for just a few jiggles, maybe, we should talk to dad, and maybe, nine-year-old Little League was not a good idea."

"Mom let's not bother Dad. Hey, here's an idea, how about I spill a coke on myself every time I go to bat. I'm left-handed people think I'm clumsy as it is, that might work."

"That's a lot of money's worth of wasted coke."

A short time passed, seemingly an eternity to each conversant or perhaps combatant, during which time, there was some staring, not at each other just into space, some distracted foot shuffling, some looking at their feet, a counting of fingers, scratching of heads, smoking of a cigarette (Mom only, of course), and other overt physical cues, perhaps, clues, each suggesting there was some high order thinking going down on each side of the field, it was not a simple problem.

Mrs. Stafford was the first to blink and to respond.

"Butchie, I think I have solved the problem."

"Mom, if there really is a problem?"

If only the Stafford family, Mrs. Stafford in particular, back then in 1960, was connected to a patent attorney, or a forward thinking Kimberly-Clarke marketing manager thrown back in time, because in the next few minutes, in her head, and over the next few hours at her sewing machine, simply using some cotton, some plastic, and few pairs of Walter's slightly yellowed in the front BVD's, Mrs. Stafford invented and produced the first prototypes for the not too soon to be invented Depend™ Adult Undergarments, in this case, the not quite adult undergarment to prevent unfortunate and embarrassing accidents, especially on the ballfield, and especially for slightly fat, extremely insecure and nervous nine-year-old Little League ballplayers. Not particularly creative, other than in the kitchen, nevertheless, natural maternal instinct, and the need to ensure her son's survival and well-being, took control of Mrs. Stafford and tapped into heretofore unknown dimensions of creativity, and those heretofore unknown dimensions provided a solution to a problem most immense. That solution being that Mrs. Stafford's youngest precocious and obese offspring, after donning her invention, his newly fashioned protective suit of armor, could fearlessly step up to the plate, and follow forth in the elder Walter's footsteps as a local baseball star.

Time passed, games were played, some were won, others lost, April turned into early June, Mom's skills were refined, hours of practice, and by all standards of measurement, Mrs. Stafford's armor did work quite well, any pee event that actually happened (and there were quite a few) seemingly went unnoticed. These 'events' went unnoticed to Butchie's team, to the opposition, to Butch's dad, to the fans, to just about everybody, cepting Butchie and his mom, of course. Encased in his protective armor, little Butch could fearlessly set forth to chase the family goal of Little League stardom, it would simply be a matter of time before records were falling, records were there for the taking.

Regrettably, hopes and desires do not reality make, and alas, stardom was not to be had, at least, not in Little League, it was just beyond the limited reach of the overweight, undersized, myopic, and slightly moist nine-year-old Walter!

The Younger was a starter, he played in every game of his nine-year-old season, most at first base. A small bragging right the younger Walter often pointed out to others, but what he didn't point out was that he was the Coach's son and perhaps, the starting line-up decisions were not always on the up and up. While a starter he was, he was not quite a star, perhaps better than average, but perhaps not. What's clear, and a posit both the author and the now older younger Walter agree upon, is that sometime in the latter part of 1950, his Dad's baseball genes exited early, at the time when Butchie's mom's egg and his dad's, Walter the Elder's sperm, decided to get together and party and this party leading to the first moments of existence for younger Walter. So much for aspirations, expectations, hopes, and dreams, at least, baseball dreams. Genetics is very complicated, but a truth to behold, should we expect the unexpected or be surprised by the expected? Seems to be a coin toss here!

In fact, it wasn't until the tenth game of the 1960 season, little Butchie's twenty-sixth at bat, that he actually lifted that massive, twenty-nine-inch, oak Louisville Slugger bat from his shoulder and took a cut at that inbound, white sphere. Perhaps, as many as one hundred and fifty pitches flew past young Butchie, most likely clocking 40-50 mph, some with far less velocity, just lobs, and he not taking a single cut. Obviously, for the first twenty-five at bats, Butchie either walked or was called out on strikes (he might have been hit by a pitch a few times, which upped his OPS), and as Butchie recalls, there were a lot of walks. This was Little League after all, a no-hitter could be pitched and still the opposing team might score eight or nine runs.

Change is a universal given, pretty much the only thing we can be sure of, and things did change and took a different track during his third at bat (his last, as it turned out) in game number ten. Everybody on Butchie's team, his opponents, fans as well, and certainly the involved parents, realized Butchie was up next and there was no doubt as to the outcome of this upcoming at bat, there would be a walk or a called strike out. The opposing pitcher was dealing strikes, so a K was likely. Whenever little Butchie came to the plate, opposing coaches would urge their pitcher to just lob the pitch over the plate, "He isn't going to swing," they would plead from the dugout. However, on this tenth game of the season, Mrs. Stafford realized the elder Walter obviously couldn't get her precious somewhat obese son to swing, so it was up to her. She solved one Butchie problem already, why not two? So, Mrs. Stafford and Butchie's sister, Bobbie, forming a not to be ignored female force, and with all the volume and power they could muster, yelled "Swing, batter batter, swing batter," as each pitch tracked towards the plate. I to this day, contend that at least one Hollywood screen writer was at this game and requisitioned for their use in the movie 'Ferris Buhler's Day Off', the chant that both Stafford family females so vehemently proclaimed throughout that at bat. Royalties may be due here!

On the third pitch of that at bat, Butchie actually lifted that 29-inch, Kentucky oak, Louisville Slugger off his shoulder and gave a mighty rip. It was a great swing, little Butchie did know how to swing, he practiced many hours perfecting a slight uppercut swing, but it was not well timed, in fact, the swing and indeed contact with the ball was made after the catcher had caught the ball and was in the process of throwing it back to the pitcher. However, practically everyone in the grandstands, the players, the coaches, and the umpire himself, were so aware that swing-less Butchie was up that the unexpected swing took everyone by surprise (no one was really watching little Butchie, why would they, he wasn't going to lift that piece of oak off his shoulder) and the fact that contact was made as the ball was being thrown back to the pitcher went largely unnoticed. Of course, the catcher did know, but the umpire who was calling the game happened to sneeze at the wrong, actually perhaps the right time and missed the play completely.

On that returning toss, back to the pitcher from the catcher, Butchie's not quite solid contact with the ball resulted in a soft dribbler hit towards third base. The ball was already on its way back to the pitcher, so the contact simply assisted the ball, increasing its velocity somewhat, and diverting the directional vector towards third base. After the swing, Butchie just stood there, amazed; he was in unchartered territories, expectations, none, no idea what to do next. Even to this very day, Butchie has no recollection of the swing or hitting the return toss back to the pitcher. A momentous quiet descended upon the field and grandstands, everyone was shocked into complete silence. Dad, his mom, and sister and likely everyone watching, obviously not the opposing team players or their fans, finally yelled in unison, *Run.* Always ready to obey a command, Butchie began his slow, fat boy run, those twenty some yards, towards first base. With plenty of time to spare, and noticing the progress or lack thereof of the painfully slow Roundabout runner, the third baseman, an experienced fielder, neatly scooped up the ball and proceeded to throw that said ball some twenty or so feet over the first baseman's head, the ball rolling to the fence about thirty feet behind first base. As Butchie approached first base, the first base coach, Bunsen, waved his arms in circles, universal code for the runner not to stop but to keep going onto second base. Butchie, now out of breath, obeyed the command and continued his tortoise-like pace towards second. The first baseman, quickly ran to the fence, retrieved the ball, and knowing with just an average toss, he could easily throw out that turtle speeding towards second, hurried his toss, and heaved that white rock far into left field. As Butchie approached second, gasping and praying he could stop here, he looked at the third base coach, his Dad, who to Butchie's more than worse imaginable nightmare, was waving his arms signaling take third. Off again.

Both, the third baseman and the left fielder, were running after the errant toss from first, so third base was open. Butchie seeing this, eased up a bit and was shuffling into third basking in celebration of his first hit a Little League triple. To his joy, his Dad was holding out both palms towards Butchie at chest level, signaling stop. Very good news as Butchie's heart rate was likely well over 200 bpm, not good for a somewhat obese nine-year-old (and probably true for just about everybody). However, as he approached the bag, just settling in, his Dad started wildly waving his arms in circles indicating, well, you know by now what that means. Apparently, the third baseman and left fielder collided with each other, going after the first baseman's errant toss and were now arguing, each with hands on the ball as to who should throw out the barely moving now even slower, the turtle reference no longer applies, Roundabout runner heading home. The third baseman won the struggle, he being the older and the alpha-male of the two, and rocketed a strike towards home, easily strong enough and on line, and if the catcher caught the ball, clearly Butchie would have been out. As it turned out, the catcher never got the chance to field the ball. Upon releasing his missile, or perhaps a second or three later, the third baseman, Butchie and the catcher were three points that made up a perfectly straight line. The ball was thrown with such force it was still about five feet off the ground as it approached the catcher, just about at center of the head height. Butchie had long ago lost his helmet at some point between first and second and was moving so slowly that he was pretty much stationary, thus, that incoming rocket from left field, that five ounce plus Rawling's official Little League baseball, impacted the back-left side of Butchie's head with a massive force, resulting in a resounding thud that could be heard by all. Obviously, there were more than a few gasps around the field and in the grandstands. Mom and sister jumped to their feet, seemingly, somewhat in fear and also to get a better look. After impact, the ball guiltlessly bounced off the back of Butchie's head, and dropped gently to the ground, as if in slow motion, well out of reach of the catcher, but of most importance, that unexpected impact, added just enough momentum to Butchie's rapidly evaporating forward motion to, in fact, propel him face first onto and completely covering home plate. Amidst the cloud of dust created by Butchie's landing (and it was quite a cloud, almost nuclear), the umpire, rushing from the rear to the front to get a better look, barely visible now enveloped within the dust, threw off his mask, rotated both arms outward one hundred eighty degrees at chest height, palms down, and after one or two coughs, managed to eke out, so all could hear, "Safe at, ahem, home!"

Within seconds of crossing (actually, falling upon) that holy isosceles right pentagon, a slightly dazed Butchie (possibly concussed), who didn't arise via his own power, was first surrounded and then lifted, hoisted into the air by a nimbus of gray uniformed teammates, jumping up and down (the jumps were *de minimis* as these young lads were hoisting quite a load) in a crazed celebration of victory, the kind only young boys (and girls) can and really should have[35].

___________________

[35] Meaningless celebrations have been taken to the extreme today by superstars and lesser heroes alike, making every game seem like the event most extraordinaire with players and fans participating in fantastical celebrations certainly more than on a nightly basis. Kirk Gibson, Bill Maseroski, Bobby Thompson, Don Larsen, these were all moments for uninhibited celebration, but today, every victory is seemingly raised to an ultimate level of worship. I guess I am fighting a lost cause as the end zone dance is now standard fare, although fines are imposed for excessive exuberance. However, point in fact, the other night in real time, a team not to be named with a record of 50-70 going nowhere, no post season chances, partied on the field, as if they just won the seventh game of the World Series. It was indeed a walk off home run, at home, winning in ten innings, 1-0, in a not your typical game. The opposing pitcher had a perfect game going into the ninth, however, the lead-off batter reached first based on an error, a not so easy play, but certainly, a gettable chance by the third baseman. The pitcher retires the next three batters easily, so he had a no hitter, almost perfect game through nine innings, at the time, a 0-0 tie. In the tenth inning, the visiting team does not score, and against the advice of the numerous announcers from ESPN, the home team's announcer, the visiting team's announcer, just about everybody everywhere, the coach sends out the no hit pitcher to pitch the tenth. In fact, the no hit guy would have had to pitch eleven innings to record the victory, as the best the visiting team could do was maintain the tie through ten and go for the win in the eleventh. Of course and you can guess what happens next, first pitch in the tenth a walk-off homerun. The no hitter gone, shut out gone, victory gone, perfect game was gone in the ninth. Of course, the home team celebrated as if there was no tomorrow and there will be no tomorrows for this hapless team,

This multilayered celebration was, in fact, paying respect to Butchie's first swing (about time), his first hit (it wasn't a hit), and his first Little League home run (nonsense, at most it in fact, should have been scored as safe on an error and taking second, third, and scoring on two additional throwing errors). Let's add to that, the fact that the swing and subsequent events would have resulted in a game winning walk-off hit as well, since the score was tied 1-1 bottom of the sixth inning (the final inning in Little League baseball).

The pandemonium, on the field and in the surrounding grandstands, ensued for at least five minutes, during which time, the crying catcher was trying to explain to his coach Dad, "Dad, I was throwing the ball back to the pitcher when he hit it, there must be some rule against that." The coach Dad knew this was true, there were rules addressing important issues such as this one, but he, the Dad, was a bit hesitant to bring it up, and put a kibosh on the revelries, so he let the celebrations continue for a few minutes. Besides,

---

as their record now 51-70 will perhaps serve the somewhat dubious purpose of keeping them out of divisional last place, perhaps, something to celebrate. Of course, after the homerun, it was mania on the field; as before stated an event most extraordinaire! The good news, the losing team is twelve games ahead of their nearest rival, on pace to set a record for most wins in the season and likely favored for a National League title at least. Added info if you are interested, in 1959, Harvey Haddocks pitched twelve perfect innings for the Pirates, retiring thirty-six Milwaukee Braves batters only to lose the game 1-0, on a Joe Adcock double in the thirteenth inning. That would seem to be another 'Oh Fuck' moment.

he wasn't sure he could get anyone to corroborate his son's account, as he, himself, was so shocked by the swing he couldn't rightly say what had happened.

The coach Dad was giving serious thought to his next step, this was after all 1960s New England youth baseball, and even at this level, winning was winning, it's not modern-day youth sports where everyone gets a participation medal. No, winning was winning and losing was not, a world of difference between the two back in 1960s western Massachusetts. However, his deep thoughts and deliberate ruminations were rudely interrupted as a fan, a former but now retired local umpire, briskly and with considerable agitation, approached the coach Dad.

"Damn it, Coach," he proclaimed as he emerged from the bleacher area, past some teary-eyed players into the dugout, "You know the ball was hit as your son was throwing it back to little Nicky (the pitcher in this case)."

"You sure about that Soapy?" asked Coach, his tone definitely dripping with hopefulness. Soapy was the nickname for this long-retired umpire, he didn't seem to mind, this sobriquet took and held after an event, many years ago, in which a team, upset with his calls during a particular game, began to inquire from the bench, "Hey, ump, do you have soap in your eyes?" these pejoratives implying his calls were off because he couldn't see straight.

Soapy, appearance-wise, was the total package, what you would expect from a former, lifetime youth baseball volunteer umpire. Military bearing, no non-sense attitude, just looking at his face, you knew acid reflux was in play. Nevertheless, he was highly respected by the baseball community during his days as an umpire and considered a selfless and honest man, concerned with community values. Among the knowing, however, there was some shock when at the relatively young age of forty-seven, he had double cataract surgery and started wearing corrective lenses, which, back in those days, due to their thickness, might have been fashioned out of recycled coke bottles. But no, all this aside, his reputation was left intact and he was considered a local expert regarding the rules of the game.

"Damn right, I'm sure, you know I've got eagle eye vision, now, it just ain't right losing a game that way," Soapy replied.

The coach Dad considered the comments, let them settle in, it took more than a few minutes, and after such deliberate considerations, approached Bunsen and elder Walter, as in the interim, the celebration still continued and in fact escalated. Someone in the stands had apparently brought some fireworks (might have confused them with their smokes, after a few beers, they begin to look alike) and purposefully or accidentally, set them off, so the level of insanity (and noise) was rising exponentially. This, of course, incited all the dogs that had been brought to the game, partly for their enjoyment, what dog doesn't enjoy a bunch of boys running around and throwing balls about, but they were also there to add their articulated support, which was considerable (both, their support and their number). This chorus incited a many other canine friend in the surrounding homes to add their unique soprano, alto, and bass, to the ruckus. A few of the Roundabout Dad's figuring the game was over and a victory declared, cracked open their coolers and were enjoying a cold Narragansett Lager, Genesee Cream Ale, a Miller's, or a Schlitz on this warm, late-spring evening, slapping each other on the back, deftly managing to talk with their hands, tend their cigarettes and drink an icy brew all at the same time. Cigarettes were bobbing up and down on their lips, as they wildly reviewed the end of the game, both hands needed for emphasis, ashes, and embers, from the burning orange torches flying through the grandstands seemingly an impromptu sequel to the earlier fireworks display.

Mom and sister, of course, knew that Butchie hit the ball as it was being thrown back to the pitcher and were just sitting there, occasionally making eye contact with each other, but no words exchanged, fingers crossed, hoping for the best, but knowing that, in all likelihood, the other shoe was about to drop metaphorically speaking.

The four dad coaches discreetly signaled for the umpire to meet with them at the third base side of the field. The celebration, in fact more of a cacophonous hullabaloo, seemed to be winding down, a bit, at least. No five-gallon Gatorade containers existed back then, so thankfully, no one, coaches, players nor fans were doused. The firework display had ceased; however, a few dads had hurried towards their cars, hard to tell if they were after more fireworks, beer, or smokes. The dogs were still agitated, perhaps their level of concern intensifying as their sixth or perhaps, seventh sense knowing something important was about to go down.

Spreading throughout the grandstands, fans, one by one, noticed, only mere seconds in arrears of their faithful canine companions, the impromptu meeting, the small confederacy of minds, that was beginning to take place over by the third base dugout. A few of the fans, likely on their third or more beers rudely and a bit too loudly exclaimed, "What the F. is going on?"

Harsh stares from moms, dads, and dogs alike.

All noticed that within the small group of coaches and umpires, plus one, the demeanor of all was quite serious, low voices, nodding heads, solemn faces, and 'mucho', macho as well, pointedly exaggerated hand waving. Some fans also noticed that Soapy was part of the meeting and a few in the grandstands commented, "What's that blind bastard doing on the field?" Apparently, he was not universally loved, but after all, who is? Unless you do absolutely nothing at all, you are bound to attract a few critics.

Within fewer than a few minutes, celebrations terminated; both, the playing field and the surrounding grandstands, quieted. A snowy, winter-like quiet enveloped the immediate area, except for a few random barks (the dogs had mostly quieted, they were just waiting), a crying baby, a small plane landing at the nearby local airport, and some low mummers and speculation among the gathered crowd, there was a shrouded quiet, but an unstable one, waiting to momentarily explode into something else. On the ballfield, the players migrated back to their respective sides of the diamond, like tiny iron shavings repositioning themselves under the force of a powerful magnet.

The six actors, orchestrating this drama, solemnly walked towards the cage behind home plate, heads down, until, in unison, six weighty faces greeted the fans. Most of the fans, pretty much parents, grandparents, uncles and aunts, and siblings (really, who else attends Little League games) had already left their seats, younger children in tow, more importantly, bringing along their beer and cigarettes, and had already gathered in that general area behind the cage. The dogs obediently followed. There were no PA systems at this field, Fetlock Park, in New Apley in 1960, loud voices were required.

No one seemed ready to speak. Soapy interjected, "It's your job, ump, tell 'em."

Hesitantly, the umpire stepped forward, distancing himself from the group. Before explaining what was going down, he proclaimed that the six of them, he, the coaches, and Soapy as well had reached a general consensus and agreement as to the game ending events. The coaches, all being very quiet, just nodding their heads, looking at each other dumbly, faces quite grim, all just waiting for this scene to play out, each one realizing this was a perfect example of a no-win situation.

The ump explained what had happened, "That the ball was hit on the catcher's throw on its way back to the pitcher and thus, was not in play, and in accordance with Little League rules, the pitch would be recorded as a strike."

The hit did not count, it never happened, there was no error assisted homerun and the score was still tied at 1-1, and Butchie was at still bat with a pitch count of two balls and one strike, still the bottom of the sixth inning with two out.

The grandstands went a bit wild, a bit being a wild understatement. Of course, at every Little League game, exactly fifty percent of the fans agree with a decision and fifty percent disagree. It's basic math.

The dogs, not caring which team won, but simply wanting justice, were sensing an atrocity was growing around them. Dogs are never happy when rules interfere with just plain old fun! In reaction to the decision, they began wildly barking and howling like coyotes, running about in circles, rudely vocalizing their contempt for this incontestably unfair decision. From the stands, a multitude of fans, clearly Roundarians, followed the dog's lead and cans of Millers and Schlitz, emptied of course, no sense wasting beer, were thrown at the ump and coaches; being emptied, they never made it to the field, too light to fly very far, basic aerodynamics. A few small fights broke out Roundabout Dad's versus Kiwanis Dad's (Kiwanis being the opposing team and another local social club), nothing substantial, just shoving, swearing, and chest pumping. Beer was spilt, cigarettes were dropped, a modest financial setback, but the ruckus was pretty tame, unlikely a Band-Aid was even required. Mothers and siblings of the players dumbly looked at each other, not knowing or caring what the outcome was, just wanting to go home. This game was becoming more than what they wanted or expected. After all, the duties of the next day were looming in front of them and rapidly approaching.

However, in the briefest of moments, the rumpus ended. Tempers cooled, fights were amicably ended, and mothers with children began heading *sans* spouses back to their station wagons. By the time the proverbial dust had settled, it was dark. Dusk comes early in the Berkshire Mountains of Western Massachusetts, so the game was called, and it was a 1-1 tie. No one was happy. Ties never make anyone happy, they are equivalent, in almost all aspects, to a loss. Because the play was called dead, in a sense, ended before it started, Butchie never got an official at bat. No strikeout, no walk, no error assisted, game winning homerun. It was as if never happened!

This was the tenth game of the Little League season in a twelve-game schedule. Ties are unheard of in Little League baseball, especially back in the 1960s in Massachusetts, and you know all this as I have already gone through the winning is winning thing-a-majig. However, being that both teams were not in playoff contention, the decision to call the game as a 1-1 tie stood. There would be no league review of the events leading to that decision nor would there be a scheduling of a date for the game to be completed; the result of the game would stand as a 1-1 tie. End of story, that story, not The Story.

********

As far as first swings go, this one was pretty amazing. The fact that it happened far too late into Butchie's Little League career, and that the play was called dead, and that it wasn't actually considered an official swing, is inconsequential and really doesn't impact the significance of the swing and the ten or fifteen minutes of insanity that ensued. Briefly, the author was considering the "The Accidental Home-Run" as the title of this narrative, however, in no sense, by any word or in any world, could Butchie's hit have been considered a homerun, and the now elder, younger Walter and the author as well agree on that, they, the two of them, both viewing life quite similarly, and from a painfully realistic, sometimes limiting and scientifically based (and definitely biased) perspective. However, what they both can completely agree on, and my guess is the same can be said for quite a few others who were there that momentous day, is that rarely, almost never, in fact, does lifting from the shoulder, especially, for the first time, that lumber, that Louisville slugger, that bat, it being made from American grown oak, twenty nine or so inches of such oak, result in such an unforgettable event.

While Butchie, seldom gets back home these days, New Apley is far more than just a few miles from his current roost, on the occasions that he does, and if recognized by any of his former teammates or long forgotten contemporaries, he often hears, sometimes shouted from across the street of this somewhat, now, less quiet, smallish American town, "Hey, Butchie, how about that first swing."

Although stricken from the official record, Butchie still considers this at bat, his first and only homerun in Little League baseball and in fact, in any of the organized baseball he played. By now, we should all be aware that reality, perceived or real, for Butchie, then and to a lesser degree now, was and is not an absolute, but often, for Butchie, a matter of preference. We, thus, must consider and factor this in, for consideration of Butchie's perhaps slightly irrational remembrances of details important and otherwise concerning the events we have painfully described in these pages.

Whenever queried the now elder Butchie, acknowledges that his freshman year in high school was the official end of his baseball playing days (coaching; now that's another story).[36] During that freshman year, Butchie

---

[36] Butchie actually came quite close to a hitting a homerun on two different occasions. The first time was in 1963, it was his last year

was still playing first base. At five feet, five inches tall, he was pretty short for the position (he was still somewhat overweight, quite slow and only a mediocre hitter, not a lot

---

in Little League, and he earned a berth on the All-Star team, perhaps, more for perseverance than talent. Nevertheless, he was the starting first baseman in that game, batting sixth. The game was played in Pittsfield, Massachusetts and in his first at bat, Butchie hit a massive shot (somewhat, for him at least) to dead center field, and it cleared the centerfield fence by perhaps five feet or more. Unfortunately, however, the ball hit dead on the flagpole, that pole bearing the US flag, the strike producing a quite loud metallic clang resonating throughout the park and surrounds and the impact causing the ball to bounce straight back into play. A ground rule double was recorded. Perhaps, this was the wrong call.

The other occasion and Butchie's last opportunity for an official homerun occurred while he was playing a JV game for Dreary Regional High School at Noble Field in New Apley in 1966, the last year he played organized baseball. The field was unbounded, there was plenty of room for other activities in this multipurpose sports park and far out in right field, a playground, swings, etc., was set up some three hundred plus feet away from home plate, much of it in foul territory, but some trespassing onto what would be considered very deep right field. During this at bat, Butchie hit a hard line-drive over the first baseman's outstretched glove, skirting well past the right fielder, who was playing quite shallow and not guarding the line, and this frozen rope (now terminology for a hard line drive) rolling seemingly forever. As Butchie was rounding third, gleefully heading for home, the umpire waved towards second base indicating a ground rule double. Regrettably a small child playing on the swings, had run onto the field, picked up the ball, and interfered with the play. Alas, the correct call here. Butchie's last chance for baseball stardom.

going for him). It's an advantage as a first baseman, to be tall, so you have a better chance at fielding errant tosses, however, despite his size, he was still considered an excellent fielder (all those golf-balls and broken windows) and this led to a lot of playing time. At the end of the season, when sophomore first baseman, Steve Dicchechio, (he actually started on the JV team but was moved up during the season to varsity) was named Captain of the varsity team for the upcoming season, Butchie realized he would never be the starting varsity first baseman, thus, that freshman year, was his final year in organized ball. As it turned out, Butchie played varsity golf his sophomore, junior, and senior years in high school, actually co-captaining the team his last year, and playing well enough in local events to make it to the regional payoffs, where he proceeded to hit three balls out of bounds from the tee on the first hole, record a ten on that dog-leg left par four, end up shooting an 82, and missing the cut for the state finals by one stroke. Apparently, a better golfer than baseball player, he, obviously, inherited some of the elder Walter's golf skills.

Later, as an adult, baseball would make a return into Butchie's life; however, by this time, he was known by all, and for many years, in fact, as Walter, perhaps, an elder Walter, but not Walter the Elder II. Although his dad had passed away some years previous, and in fact, the now older Younger did have a son, that son was not another Walter, another non-tradition thus started, his son was named Garret. Like his dad, Walter (aka Butchie), did get involved in baseball following in his Dad's footsteps, becoming a local coach, coaching his son for three years of Little League baseball, and two years of Babe Ruth ball with friend Kevin, the Fireman! Both, Kevin and Butchie, along with their son's, had quite a few dad-son baseball adventures, most forgettable, some stretching to its limits, the durability of the father-son bond, but a few, very special and those special occasions, perhaps, worthy of additional narration. Both their sons played and, in fact, excelled on those teams. By the time Garret was fifteen, his baseball skills had far surpassed any his Dad had, perhaps, more so than the elder Walter as well, hard to compare talents separated by so many years, and at the point in time, when throwing batting practice to his son could actually be a danger for the older younger Walter, both decided it was time to let Garret move on, on his own, and he did. Thus, while Garret, outdoing his dad, continued to play ball throughout high school, it was without his dad's coaching, but certainly, it was with his Dad's support. While neither Garret nor Kevin's son, Jeff, required their mom's to construct protective 'undergarments' to ward off demons of the psyche, Garret would play a more than minor role in another adventure concerning baseball garments, one, in which, his best friend, Weston, experienced a life altering event, all because of a pair of baseball pants. But that's another time and another story.

# Part 7

## Epilogue: A few days after the first swing

**First Dialog—Bunsen and Elder Walter**

Bunsen, "Give me one, come on cough it up."

Elder, "What?"

Bunsen, "A fag!"

Elder, "You're too young to use that term. You were in fuckin diapers when I was in England jumping into ditches avoiding those fuckin V1, goddamn buzz bombs lobbed over the Channel by the fuckin Krauts. You lucky shit, you avoided, both, Korea and Vietnam, won the draft lottery, fuck you. The luck of a fucking birthday."

Bunsen, "Well it didn't hurt you any and from what I hear, drinking and screwing was you all you did over there, and jumping, no, my guess is falling shit-faced drunk into ditches, whether you heard a V1 or not. And speaking of diapers, *your son is still in fuckin diapers*! Come on hand it over."

Elder, "Ain't it the sad fuckin truth, the diapers, I mean, and yeah, I do admit your WWII assessment was right on!

Hey, he finally swung at a fuckin pitch, ain't that something."

Bunsen, "Yeah, I know, I was there, remember, I waved him onto second base."

Elder, "True, so true. Hey, for a minute, I thought the homerun was going to stand, until Soapy butted in."

Bunsen, "It was never a home run. Cig?"

Elder, "Nother beer?"

Bunsen, "Sure!"

Elder, "True, it wasn't. But what the fuck, it would have been a great finish to a great fuckin game."

Bunsen, "Lots of what ifs, right! Hey, here's another what if; I'm investing in a bowling alley, gonna be open pretty soon. Wanna be a partner? Gonna be amazing, lots of dough!"

Elder, "Bowling in New Apley, seriously? I think I'll pass. Bunsen, sometimes, I really don't—"

Bunsen, "Your loss. Hey, you know you can drink, bowl, and smoke all at once; the Triple Crown me thinks!"

Elder, "When you put it that way, but no, Tootsie, no can't even bring it up."

Bunsen, "Well, your loss. You gonna re-up for coaching next year?"

Elder, "Gotta. He won't survive, they will kill him if I'm not there. You know, sometimes, I think there was a mix up at the fuckin hospital! Hope he loses the diaper!"

Bunsen, "True, now give me that fag!"

# Dialog 2—Mrs. Stafford and Madge

Mrs. Stafford, "I finally couldn't take anymore, so Bobbie and I just started yelling, "Swing, Swing, Swing.""

M, "And did he?"

Mrs. Stafford, "Yeah, after three or four pitches. I guess he was too embarrassed not to."

M, "How did your sewing skills hold up?"

Mrs. Stafford, "Mother of Christ, thank god, working perfectly no one knows, 'cept you, of course."

M, "Not a word."

Mrs. Stafford, "Yeah, so, he finally hit the ball, solid contact, beat it out and then pretty much stole second and third base and home as well. Game winning hit."

M, "That's amazing, he's pretty fast for someone that f— I mean that small."

Mrs. Stafford, "Yeah, he sure is, but then, the goddamn umpire called the play dead cuz of some stupit rule."

M, "Those umps they suck for sure; they all play favorites."

Mrs. Stafford, "Can't believe he still needs that stupit diaper, I thought just the idea of having it would stop the problem, but that sure ain't the case. Seems like he needs it more and more, the more he wears it. Maybe, I should start a business, but really who else needs such things, seriously, diapers for grown-ups."

M, "Crazy idea for sure, but wait a minute, wait a minute, my gramps, no, no never mind, silly thought. Butchie sure doesn't have your moxie, does he?"

Mrs. Stafford, "Sadly not! You know and don't repeat this, but, sometimes, I feel like there might have been a mix up at the hospital."

M, "Ain't it the truth."

## Dialog 3—Hymie and The Younger Walter

Hymie, "Hey, fat boy!"

Younger Walter, "Hey, *hebe* man!"

Hymie, "What's new, as if there ever is?"

Younger Walter, "I actually have some amazing news. I hit my first home run a couple of days ago."

Hymie, "Sure, really? Maybe, no doubtful. Now, wait, wait a sec, I seem to recall and I don't play ball, so I might be wrong, but don't you actually have to swing the bat to hit a home run? What happened, did you get hit by the same pitch four times and they awarded you four bases?"

Younger Walter, "Hilarious, you should consider a stand-up career, but a Jew comedian, no, no way, heck, it's only 1960! So, for your edification, (look it up, if you have to) I finally swung (or is it 'swang', verb tenses confuse me). I decided it was time for lumber lift-off, even though my OBP was well over 700 with walks and whatnot. I'm in a rarified zone saber-metrically speaking."

Hymie, "So, you better give me the details but keep it short."

Younger Walter, "Hit a dribbler, beat it out, just kept running, they couldn't get me out."

Hymie, "Yeah, you are known for your speed!"

Younger Walter, "I see quite a few more home runs in my future, doesn't seem that hard really."

Hymie, "Hey, speaking of fiction, got some new books, this Brit guy, Fleming, I hear some are pretty racy, some good sex scenes, let's hit the library."

Younger Walter, "Good idea. I gotta pick up a book about field dressing a deer for Uncle Al, anyway."

Hymie, "Yeah, so speaking of your Uncle Al, and believe me I'd rather not, but I actually ran into your Uncle Al downtown a few days ago, pretty frackin' scary is all I can say, he was actually having a conversation with a parking meter, a friend of his is my guess! You sure you weren't adopted?"

## Dialog 4—Opposing Coach Dad and Catcher Son

Dad, "Fucking unbelievable, that fat little fucker in a diaper hits the ball on your fuckin throwback to the fuckin pitcher and starts to haul his fuckin fat little piss splattered ass around the bases and thinks he hit a fuckin homerun. As I said fuckin amazing!"

Son, "Fucking right, dad!"

Dad, "What a fuckin loser, the whole family, in fact. They think no one knows about the diaper. Son, I tell you that kid is gonna be cutting your fuckin lawn thirty fuckin years from today, mark my fuckin words!"

Son, "Fucking right!"

Dad, "Son, I told you not to say fuck in the house, your mom might hear!"

Son, "Sorry, Dad."

## Monologue Last—Soapy

Soapy, "Where the fuck are my glasses?"

**The End-Sort Of**